Margaret Oliphant

A house in Bloomsbury

A Novel. Vol. 2

Margaret Oliphant

A house in Bloomsbury
A Novel. Vol. 2

ISBN/EAN: 9783337273644

Printed in Europe, USA, Canada, Australia, Japan

Cover: Foto ©Andreas Hilbeck / pixelio.de

More available books at **www.hansebooks.com**

A HOUSE IN BLOOMSBURY

A NOVEL

BY

Mrs. OLIPHANT

VOL. II.

London

HUTCHINSON & CO.

34 PATERNOSTER ROW, E.C.

1894

A HOUSE IN BLOOMSBURY.

CHAPTER XIV.

"No, Mannering," said Dr. Roland, "I can't say that you may go back to the Museum in a week. I don't know when you will be up to going. I should think you had a good right to a long holiday after working there for so many years."

"Not so many years," said Mr. Mannering, "since the long break which you know of, Roland."

"In the interest of science," cried the doctor.

The patient shook his head with a melancholy smile. "Not in my own at least," he said.

"Well, it is unnecessary to discuss that question. Back you cannot go, my good fellow, till you have recovered your strength to a very different point from that you are at now. You can't go till after you've had a change. At present you're nothing but a bundle of tendencies ready to develop into anything bad that's going. That must be stopped in the first place, and you must have sea air, or mountain air, or country air, whichever you fancy. I won't be dogmatic about the kind, but the thing you must have."

" Impossible, impossible, impossible ! " Mannering had begun to cry out while the other was speaking. " Why, man, you're raving," he said. " I—so accustomed to the air of Bloomsbury, and that especially fine sort which is to be had at the Museum, that I couldn't breathe any other—I to have mountain air or sea air or country air! Nonsense! Any of them would stifle me in a couple of days."

" You will have your say, of course. And you are a great scientific gent, I'm aware ; but you know as little about your own health and what it wants as this child with her message. Well, Janie, what is it, you constant bother? Mr. Mannering? Take it to Miss Bethune, or wait till Miss Dora comes back."

" Please, sir, the gentleman is waiting, and he says he won't go till he's pyed."

" You little ass!" said the doctor. " What do you mean by coming with your ridiculous stories here?"

Mannering stretched out his thin hand and took the paper. " You see," he said, with a faint laugh, " how right I was when I said I would have nothing to do with your changes of air. It is all that my pay will do to settle my bills, and no overplus for such vanities."

" Nonsense, Mannering! The money will be forthcoming when it is known to be necessary."

"From what quarter, I should be glad to hear? Do you think the Museum will grant me a premium for staying away, for being of no use? Not very likely! I shall not be left in the lurch; they will grant me three months' holiday, or even six months' holiday, and my salary as usual. But we shall have to reduce our expenses, Dora and I, and to live as quietly as possible, instead of going off like millionaires to revel upon fresh tipples of fancy air. No, no, nothing of the kind. And, besides, I don't believe in them. I have made myself, as the French say, to the air of Blooms-bury, and in that I shall live or die."

"You don't speak at all, my dear fellow, like the man of sense you are," said the doctor. "For-tunately, I can carry things with a high hand. When I open my mouth let no patient venture to contradict. You are going away to the country now. If you don't conform to my rules, I am not at all sure I may not go further, and ordain that there is to be no work for six months, a winter on the Riviera, and so forth. I have got all these pains and penalties in my hand."

"Better and better," said Mannering, "a palace to live in, and a *chef* to cook for us, and our dinner off gold plate every day."

"There is no telling what I may do if you put me to it," Dr. Roland said, with a laugh. "But seriously, if it were my last word, you must get out of London. Nothing that you can do or say will save you from that."

"We shall see," said Mr. Mannering. "The sovereign power of an empty purse does great wonders. But here is Dora back, and without the big book, I am glad to see. What did Fiddler say?"

"I will tell you afterwards, father," said Dora, developing suddenly a little proper pride.

"Nonsense! You can tell me now—that he had two or three people in his pocket who would have bought it willingly if he had not reserved it for me, and that it was a book that nobody wanted, and would be a drug on his hands."

"Oh, father, how clever you are! That was

exactly what he said : and I did not point out
that he was contradicting himself, for fear it should
make him angry.   But he did not mind me.   He
said he could trust Mr. Mannering of the Museum;
he was quite sure he should get paid ; and he is
sending it back by one of the young men, because
it was too heavy for me."

"My poor little girl ! I ought to have known
it would be too heavy for you."

"Oh, never mind," said Dora. "I only
carried it half the way.   It was getting very heavy
indeed, I will not deny, when I met Mr. Gordon,
and he carried it for me to Fiddler's shop."

"Who is Mr. Gordon ? " said Mr. Mannering,
raising his head.

"He is a friend of Miss Bethune's," said Dora,
with something of hesitation in her voice which
struck her father's ear.

Dr. Roland looked very straight before him,
taking care to make no comment, and not to

meet Dora's eye.　There was a tacit understanding between them now on several subjects, which
the invalid felt vaguely, but could not explain to
himself.　Fortunately, however, it had not even
occurred to him that there was anything more
remarkable in the fact of a young man, met at
hazard, carrying Dora's book for her, than if the
civility had been shown to himself.

"You see," he said, "it is painful to have to
make you aware of all my indiscretions, Roland.
What has a man to do with rare editions, who
has a small income and an only child like mine?
The only thing is," he added, with a short laugh,
"they should bring their price when they come to
the hammer,—that has always been my consolation."

"They are not coming to the hammer just
yet," said the doctor.　He possessed himself
furtively, but carelessly, of the piece of paper on
the table—the bill which, as Janie said, was

wanted by a gentleman waiting downstairs. "You just manage to get over this thing, Mannering," he said, in an ingratiating tone, "and I'll promise you a long bill of health and plenty of time to make up all your lost way. You don't live in the same house with a doctor for nothing. I have been waiting for this for a long time. I could have told Vereker exactly what course it would take if he hadn't been an ass, as all these successful men are. He did take a hint or two in spite of himself; for a profession is too much for a man, it gives a certain fictitious sense in some cases, even when he is an ass. Well, Mannering, of course I couldn't prophesy what the end would be. You might have succumbed. With your habits, I thought it not unlikely."

"You cold-blooded practitioner! And what do you mean by my habits? I'm not a toper or a reveller by night."

"You are almost worse. You are a man of

the Museum, drinking in bad air night and day, and never moving from your books when you can help it. It was ten to one against you ; but some of you smoke-dried, gas-scented fellows have the devil's own constitution, and you've pulled through."

"Yes," said Mannering, holding up his thin hand to the light, and thrusting forth a long spindle-shank of a leg, "I've pulled through—as much as is left of me. It isn't a great deal to brag of."

"Having done that, with proper care I don't see why you shouldn't have a long spell of health before you—as much health as a man can expect who despises all the laws of nature—and attain a very respectable age before you die."

"Here's promises !" said Mannering. He paused and laughed, and then added in a lower tone : "Do you think that's so very desirable, after all ?"

"Most men like it," said the doctor ; "or, at

least, think they do. And for you, who have Dora to think of ——"

" Yes, there's Dora," the patient said as if to himself.

" That being the case, you are not your own property, don't you see? You have got to take care of yourself, whether you will or not. You have got to make life livable, now that it's handed back to you. It's a responsibility, like another. Having had it handed back to you, as I say, and being comparatively a young man—what are you, fifty ? "

" Thereabout; not what you would call the flower of youth."

" But a very practical, not disagreeable age— good for a great deal yet, if you treat it fairly ; but, mind you, capable of giving you a great deal of annoyance, a great deal of trouble, if you don't."

" No more before the child," said Mannering

hastily. "We must cut our coat according to our cloth, but she need not be in all our secrets. What! turtle-soup again? Am I to be made an alderman of in spite of myself? No more of this, Hal, if you love me," he said, shaking his gaunt head at the doctor, who was already disappearing downstairs.

Dr. Roland turned back to nod encouragingly to Dora, and to say : "All right, my dear ; keep it up !" But his countenance changed as he turned away again, and when he had knocked and been admitted at Miss Bethune's door, it was with a melancholy face, and a look of the greatest despondency, that he flung himself into the nearest chair.

"It will be all of no use," he cried,—"of no use, if we can't manage means and possibilities to pack them off somewhere. He will not hear of it! Wants to go back to the Museum next week—in July !—and to go on in Bloomsbury all the year, as if he had not been within a straw's breadth of his life."

"I was afraid of that," said Miss Bethune, shaking her head.

"He ought to go to the country now," said the doctor, "then to the sea, and before the coming on of winter go abroad. That's the only programme for him. He ought to be a year away. Then he might come back to the Museum like a giant refreshed, and probably write some book, or make some discovery, or do some scientific business, that would crown him with glory, and cover all the expenses; but the obstinate beast will not see it. Upon my word!" cried Dr. Roland, "I wish there could be made a decree that only women should have the big illnesses; they have such faith in a doctor's word, and such a scorn of possibilities : it always does them good to order them something that can't be done, and then do it in face of everything

—that's what I should like for the good of the race."

"I can't say much for the good of the race," said Miss Bethune ; " but you'd easily find some poor wretch of a woman that would do it for the sake of some ungrateful brute of a man."

"Ah, we haven't come to that yet," said the doctor regretfully ; " the vicarious principle has not gone so far. If it had I daresay there would be plenty of poor wretches ready to bear their neighbours' woes for a consideration. The simple rules of supply and demand would be enough to provide us proxies without any stronger senti-ment : but philosophising won't do us any good ; it won't coin money, or if it could, would not drop it into his pocket, which after all is the chief difficulty. He is not to be taken in any longer by your fictions about friendly offerings and cheap purchases. Here is a bill which that little anæmic nuisance Janie brought in, with word that a gentleman was 'wyaiting' for the payment."

"We'll send for the gentleman, and settle it," said Miss Bethune quietly, "and then it can't come up to shame us again."

The gentleman sent for turned up slowly, and came in with reluctance, keeping his face as much as possible averted. He was, however, too easily recognisable to make this contrivance available.

"Why, Hesketh, have you taken service with Fortnum and Mason?" the doctor cried.

"I'm in a trade protection office, sir," said Hesketh. "I collect bills for parties." He spoke with his eyes fixed on a distant corner, avoiding as much as possible every glance.

"In a trade protection office? And you mean to tell me that Fortnum and Mason, before even the season is over, collect their bills in this way?"

"They don't have not to say so many

customers in Bloomsbury, sir," said the young man, with that quickly-conceived impudence which is so powerful a weapon, and so congenial to his race.

"Confound their insolence! I have a good mind to go myself and give them a bit of my mind," cried Dr. Roland. "Bloomsbury has more sense, it seems, than I gave it credit for, and your pampered tradesman more impudence."

"I would just do that," said Miss Bethune. "And will it be long since you took to this trade protection, young man?—for Gilchrist brought me word you were ill in your bed not a week ago."

"A man can't stay in bed, when 'e has a wife to support, and with no 'ealth to speak of," Hesketh replied, with a little bravado; but he was very pale, and wiped the unwholesome dews from his forehead.

"Anæmia, body and soul," said the doctor to the lady, in an undertone.

"You'll come to his grandfather again in a moment," said the lady to the doctor. "Now, my lad, you shall just listen to me. Put down this moment your trade protections, and all your devices. Did you not hear, by Gilchrist, that we were meaning to give you a new chance? Not for your sake, but for your wife's, though she probably is just tarred with the same stick. We were meaning to set you up in a little shop in a quiet suburb."

Here the young fellow made a grimace, but recollected himself, and said no word.

"Eh!" cried Miss Bethune, "that wouldn't serve your purposes, my fine gentleman?"

"I never said so," said the young man. "It's awfully kind of you. Still, as I've got a place on my own hook, as it were—not that we mightn't combine the two, my wife and I. She ain't a bad

saleswoman," he added, with condescension.
"We was in the same house of business before
we was married—not that beastly old shop where
they do nothing but take away the young gentlemen's and young ladies' characters. It's as true
as life what I say. Ask any one that has ever
been there."

"Anæmia," said Miss Bethune to the doctor,
aside, "would not be proof enough, if there were
facts on the other hand."

"I always mistrust facts," the doctor replied.

"Here is your money," she resumed. "Write
me out the receipt, or rather, put your name to it.
Now mind this, I will help you if you're meaning
to do well; but if I find out anything wrong in
this, or hear that you're in bed again to-morrow,
and not fit to lift your head ——"

"No man can answer for his health," said
young Hesketh solemnly. "I may be bad, I
may be dead to-morrow, for anything I can tell."

" That is true."

" And my poor wife a widder, and the poor baby not born."

" In these circumstances," said Dr. Roland, " we'll forgive her for what wasn't her fault, and look after her. But that's not likely, unless you are fool enough to let yourself be run over, or something of that sort, going out from here."

" Which I won't, sir, if I can help it."

" And no great loss, either," the doctor said in his undertone. He watched the payment grimly, and noticed that the young man's hand shook in signing the receipt. What was the meaning of it? He sat for a moment in silence, while Hesketh's steps, quickening as he went farther off, were heard going downstairs and towards the door. " I wish I were as sure that money would find its way to the pockets of Fortnum and Mason, as I am that yonder down-looking hound had a criminal grandfather," he said.

" Well, there is the receipt, anyhow. Will you go and inquire ? "

" To what good ? There would be a great fuss, and the young fool would get into prison probably ; whereas we may still hope that it is all right, and that he has turned over a new leaf."

" I should not be content without being at the bottom of it," said Miss Bethune ; and then, after a pause : " There is another thing. The lady from South America that was here has been taken ill, Dr. Roland."

" Ah, so !" cried the doctor. " I should like to go and see her."

" You are not wanted to go and see her. It is I—which you will be surprised at—that is wanted, or, rather, Dora with me. I have had an anxious pleader here, imploring me by all that I hold dear. You will say that is not much, doctor."

" I will say nothing of the kind. But I have

little confidence in that lady from South America, or her young man."

"The young man is just as fine a young fellow! Doubt as you like, there is no deceit about him ; a countenance like the day, and eyes that meet you fair, look at him as you please. Doctor," said Miss Bethune, faltering a little, "I have taken a great notion into my head that he may turn out to be a near relation of my own."

"A relation of yours?" cried Dr. Roland, suppressing a whistle of astonishment. "My thoughts were going a very different way."

"I know, and your thoughts are justified. The lady did not conceal that she was Mrs. Mannering's sister : but the one thing does not hinder the other."

"It would be a very curious coincidence— stranger, even, than usual."

"Everything that's strange is usual," cried

Miss Bethune vehemently. "It is we that have no eyes to see."

"Perhaps," said the doctor, who loved a paradox. "I tell you what," he added briskly, "let me go and see this lady. I am very suspicious about her. I should like to make her out a little before risking it for Dora, even with you."

"You think, perhaps, you would make it out better than I should," said Miss Bethune, with some scorn. "Well, there is no saying. You would, no doubt, make out what is the matter with her, which is always the first thing that interests you."

"It explains most things, when you know how to read it," the doctor said; but in this point his opponent did not give in to him, it is hardly necessary to say. She was very much interested about Dora, but she was still more interested in the question which moved her own heart so deeply. The lady from South America might be in command of many facts on that point; and prudence seemed to argue that it was best to see and understand a little more about her first, before taking Dora, without her father's knowledge, to a stranger who made such a claim upon her.

"Though if it is her mother's sister, I don't know who could have a stronger claim upon her," said Miss Bethune.

"Provided her mother had a sister," the doctor said.

CHAPTER XV.

Miss Bethune set out accordingly, without saying anything further, to see the invalid. She took nobody into her confidence, not even Gilchrist, who had much offended her mistress by her scepticism. Much as she was interested in every unusual chain of circumstances, and much more still in anything happening to Dora Mannering, there was a still stronger impulse of personal feeling in her present expedition. It had gone to her head like wine; her eyes shone, and there was a nervous energy in every line of her tall figure in its middle-aged boniness and hardness. She walked quickly, pushing her way forward when there was any crowd with an unconscious movement, as of a strong swimmer dividing the waves. Her mind was tracing out every line of the supposed process of

(23)

events known to herself alone. It was her own story, and such a strange one as occurs seldom in the almost endless variety of strange stories that are about the world—a story of secret marriage, secret birth, and sudden overwhelming calamity. She had as a young woman given herself foolishly and hastily to an adventurer: for she was an heiress, if she continued to please an old uncle who had her fate in his hands. The news of the unexpected approach of this old man brought the sudden crisis. The husband, who had been near her in the profound quiet of the country, fled, taking with him the child, and after that no more. The marriage was altogether unknown, except to Gilchrist, and a couple of old servants in the small secluded country-house where the strange little tragedy had taken place ; and the young wife, who had never borne her husband's name, came to life again after a long illness, to find every trace of her piteous story, and of the fate of the man for

whom she had risked so much, and the child
whom she had scarcely seen, obliterated. The
agony through which she had lived in that first
period of dismay and despair, the wild secret
inquiries set on foot with so little knowledge of
how to do anything of the kind, chiefly by means
of the good and devoted Gilchrist, who, however,
knew still less even than her mistress the way to
do it—the long, monotonous years of living with
the old uncle to whom that forlorn young woman
in her secret anguish had to be nurse and companion ; the dreadful freedom afterwards, when
the fortune was hers, and the liberty so long
desired—but still no clue, no knowledge whether
the child on whom she had set her passionate
heart existed or not. The hero, the husband,
existed no longer in her imagination. That first
year of furtive fatal intercourse had revealed him
in his true colours as an adventurer, whose aim
had been her fortune. But why had he not

revealed himself when that fortune was secure?
Why had he not brought back the child who
would have secured his hold over her whatever
had happened? These questions had been discussed between Miss Bethune and her maid, till
there was no longer any contingency, any com-
bination of things or theories possible, which had
not been torn to pieces between them, with
reasonings sometimes as acute as mother's wit
could make them, sometimes as foolish as ignorance and inexperience suggested.

They had roamed all over the world in an
anxious quest after the fugitives who had disappeared so completely into the darkness. What
wind drifted them to Bloomsbury it would be too
long to inquire-ho The wife of one furtive and
troubled year, the mother of one anxious but
heavenly week, had long, long ago settled into
the angular, middle-aged unmarried lady of Mrs.
Simcox's first floor. She had dropped all her

former friends, all the people who knew about her. And those people who once knew her by her Christian name, and as they thought every incident in her life, in reality knew nothing, not a syllable of the brief romance and tragedy which formed its centre. She had developed, they all thought, into one of those eccentrics who are so often to be found in the loneliness of solitary life, odd as were all the Bethunes, with something added that was especially her own. By intervals an old friend would appear to visit her, marvelling much at the London lodging in which the mistress of more than one old comfortable house had chosen to bury herself. But the Bethunes were all queer, these visitors said ; there was a bee in their bonnet, there was a screwcrose somewhere. It is astonishing the number of Scotch families of whom this is said to account for everything their descendants may think or do.

This was the woman who marched along the

hot July streets with the same vibration of impulse
and energy which had on several occasions led her
half over the world. She had been disappointed a
thousand times, but never given up hope; and each
new will-o'-the-wisp which had led her astray had
been welcomed with the same strong confidence,
the same ever-living hope. Few of them, she ac-
knowledged to herself now, had possessed half the
likelihood of this; and every new point of certitude
grew and expanded within her as she proceeded on
her way. The same age, the same name (more or
less), a likeness which Gilchrist, fool that she was,
would not see; and then the story, proving everything of the mother who was alive but unknown.

Could anything be more certain? Miss
Bethune's progress through the streets was
more like that of a bird on the wing, with that
floating movement which is so full at once of
strength and of repose, and wings ever ready for
a swift *coup* to increase the impulse and clear the

way, than of a pedestrian walking along a hot pave-
ment. A strange coincidence! Yes, it would be a
very strange coincidence if her own very unusual
story and that of the poor Mannerings should
thus be twined together. But why should it not
be so? Truth is stranger than fiction. The
most marvellous combinations happen every day.
The stranger things are, the more likely they
are to happen. This was what she kept saying
to herself as she hurried upon her way.

She was received in the darkened room, in
the hot atmosphere perfumed and damped by the
spray of some essence, where at first Miss Bethune
felt she could scarcely breathe. When she was
brought in, in the gleam of light made by the
opened door, there was a little scream of eagerness
from the bed at the other end of the long room,
and then a cry: "But Dora? Where is Dora?
It is Dora, Dora, I want!" in a voice of disappointment and irritation close to tears.

"You must not be vexed that I came first by myself," Miss Bethune said. "To bring Dora without her father's knowledge is a strong step."

"But I have a right—I have a right!" cried the sick woman. "Nobody—not even he—could deny me a sight of her. I've hungered for years for a sight of her, and now that I am free I am going to die."

"No, no! don't say that," said Miss Bethune, with the natural instinct of denying that conclusion. "You must not let your heart go down, for that is the worst of all."

"It is perhaps the best, too," said the patient. "What could I have done? Always longing for her, never able to have her except by stealth, frightened always that she would find out, or that he should find out. Oh, no, it's better as it is. Now I can provide for my dear, and nobody to say a word. Now I can show her how I love her. And she will not judge me. A child like that doesn't judge. She will learn to pity her poor, poor —— Oh, why didn't you bring me my Dora? I may not live another day."

In the darkness, to which her eyes gradually became accustomed, Miss Bethune consulted silently with a look the attendant by the bed; and receiving from her the slight, scarcely distinguishable, answer of a shake of the head, took the sufferer's hand, and pressed it in her own.

"I will bring her," she said, "to-night, if you wish it, or to-morrow. I give you my word. If you think of yourself like that, whether you are right or not, I am not the one to disappoint you. To-night, if you wish it."

"Oh, to-night, to-night! I'll surely live till to-night," the poor woman cried.

"And many nights more, if you will only keep quite quiet, ma'am. It depends upon yourself," said the maid.

"They always tell you," said Mrs. Bristow,

" to keep quiet, as if that was the easiest thing to do. I might get up and walk all the long way to see my child ; but to be quiet without her—that is what is impossible—and knowing that perhaps I may never see her again ! "

" You shall—you shall," said Miss Bethune soothingly. " But you have a child, and a good child—a son, or as like a son as possible."

" I a son ? Oh, no, no— none but Dora ! No one I love but Dora." The poor lady paused then with a sob, and said in a changed voice : " You mean Harry Gordon ? Oh, it is easy to see you are not a mother. He is very good—oh, very good. He was adopted by Mr. Bristow. Oh," she cried, with a long crying breath, " Mr. Bristow ought to have done something for Harry. He ought to—I always said so. I did not want to have everything left to me."

She wrung her thin hands, and a convulsive sob came out of the darkness.

" Ma'am," said the maid, " I must send this lady away, and put a stop to everything, if you get agitated like this."

" I'll be quite calm, Miller—quite calm," the patient cried, putting out her hand and clutching Miss Bethune's dress.

" To keep her calm I will talk to her of this other subject," said Miss Bethune, with an injured tone in her voice. She held her head high, elevating her spare figure, as if in disdain. " Let us forget Dora for the moment," she said, " and speak of this young man that has only been a son to you for the most of his life, only given you his affection and his services and everything a child could do—but is nothing, of course, in comparison with a little girl you know nothing about, who is your niece in blood."

" Oh, my niece, my niece !" the poor lady murmured under her breath.

" Tell me something about this Harry Gordon;

it will let your mind down from the more exciting subject," said Miss Bethune, still with great dignity, as if of an offended person. " He has lived with you for years. He has shared your secrets."

" I have talked to him about Dora," she faltered.

" But yet," said the stern questioner, more and more severely, "it does not seem you have cared anything about him all these years?"

" Oh, don't say that! I have always been fond of him, always—always! He will never say I have not been kind to him," the invalid cried.

" Kind?" cried Miss Bethune, with an indignation and scorn which nothing could exceed. Then she added more gently, but with still the injured tone in her voice : " Will you tell me something about him ? It will calm you down. I take an interest in the young man. He is like somebody I once knew, and his name recalls ——"

" Perhaps you knew his father ? " said Mrs. Bristow.

" Perhaps. I would like to hear more particulars. He tells me his mother is living."

" The father was very foolish to tell him. Mr. Bristow always said so. It was on his deathbed. I suppose," cried the poor lady, with a deep sigh, "that on your deathbed you feel that you must tell everything. Oh, I've been silent, silent, so long! I feel that too. She is not a mother that it would ever be good for him to find. Mr. Bristow wished him never to come back to England, only for that. He said better be ignorant—better know nothing."

" And why was the poor mother so easily condemned ? "

" You would be shocked—you an unmarried lady—if I told you the story. She left him just after the boy was born. She fell from one degradation to another. He sent her money as long as he could keep any trace of her.   Poor, poor man ! "

" And his friends took everything for gospel that this man said ? "

" He was an honest man.   Why should he tell Mr. Bristow a lie ?   I said it was to be kept from poor Harry.   It would only make him miserable.   But there was no doubt about the truth of it—oh, none."

" I tell you," cried Miss Bethune, " that there is every doubt of it.   His mother was a poor deceived girl, that was abandoned, deserted, left to bear her misery as she could."

" Did you know his mother ? " said the patient, showing out of the darkness the gleam of eyes widened by astonishment.

" It does not matter," cried Miss Bethune.   " I know this, that the marriage was in secret, and the boy was born in secret ; and while she was ill and weak there came the news of some one coming that might leave her penniless ; and for the sake of the money, the wretched money, this man took the child up in his arms out of her very bed, and carried it away."

The sick woman clutched the arm of the other, who sat by her side, tragic and passionate, the words coming from her lips like sobs. "Oh, my poor lady," she said, "if that is your story ! But it was not that. My husband, Mr. Bristow, knew. He knew all about Gordon from the beginning. It was no secret to him. He did not take the child away till the mother had gone, till he had tried every way to find her, even to bring her back. He was a merciful man. I knew him too. Oh, poor woman, poor woman, my heart breaks for that other you knew. She is like me, she is worse off than me : but the one you know was not Harry's mother—oh, no, no—Harry's mother! If she is living it is—it is—in misery, and worse than misery."

"He said," uttered a hoarse voice, breathless, out of the dimness, which nobody could have recognised for Miss Bethune's, "that you said there was no such woman."

"I did—to comfort him, to make him believe that it was not true."

"By a lie! And such a lie—a shameful lie, when you knew so different! And how should any one believe now a word you say?"

"Oh, don't let her say such things to me, Miller, Miller!" cried the patient, with the cry of a sick child.

"Madam," said the maid, "she's very bad, as you see, and you're making her every minute worse. You can see it yourself. It's my duty to ask you to go away."

Miss Bethune rose from the side of the bed like a ghost, tall and stern, and towering over the agitated, weeping woman who lay back on the white pillows, holding out supplicating hands and

panting for breath. She stood for a moment looking as if she would have taken her by the throat.
Then she gave herself a little shake, and turned
away.

Once more the invalid clutched at her dress
and drew her back. "Oh," she cried, "have
mercy upon me! Don't go away—don't go
away! I will bear anything. Say what you like,
but bring me Dora—bring me Dora—before I die."

"Why should I bring you Dora? Me to
whom nobody brings —— What is it to me if you
live or if you die?"

"Oh, bring me Dora—bring me Dora!" the
poor woman wailed, holding fast by her visitor's
dress. She flung herself half out of the bed,
drawing towards her with all her little force the
unwilling, resisting figure. "Oh, for the sake of
all you wish for yourself, bring me Dora—Dora
—before I die!"

"What have you left me to wish for?" cried

the other woman ; and she drew her skirts out of the patient's grasp.

No more different being from her who had entered an hour before by the long passages and staircases of the great hotel could have been than she who now repassed through them, looking neither to the right nor to the left—a woman like a straight line of motion and energy, as strong and stiff as iron, with expression banished from her face, and elasticity from her figure. She went back by the same streets she had come by, making her way straight through the crowd, which seemed to yield before the strength of passion and pain that was in her. There was a singing in her ears, and a buzzing in her head, and her heart was in her breast as if it had been turned to stone. Oh, she was not at her first shock of disappointment and despair. She had experienced it before; but never, she thought, in such terrible sort as now. She had so wrapped herself in this dream, which

had been suggested to her by nothing but her
own heart, what she thought her instinct, a sudden
flash of divination, the voice of nature. She had
felt sure of it the first glimpse she had of him,
before he had even told her his name. She had
been sure that this time it was the voice of nature,
that intuition of a mother which could not be deceived. So many likenesses seemed to meet in
Harry Gordon's face, so many circumstances to
combine in establishing the likelihood, at least,
that this was he. South America, the very ideal
place for an adventurer, and the strange fact that
he had a mother living whom he did not know.
A mother living! These words made a thrill of
passion, of opposition, of unmoved and immovable
conviction, rush through all her veins. A mother
living! Who could that be but she? What
would such a man care—a man who had abandoned
his wife at the moment of a woman's greatest
weakness, and taken her child from her when she

was helpless to resist him—for the ruin of her reputation after, for fixing upon her, among those who knew her not, the character of a profligate? He who had done the first, why should he hesitate to say the last? The one thing cost him trouble, the other none. It was easier to believe that than to give up what she concluded with certainty was her last hope.

Gilchrist, who had seen her coming, rushed downstairs to open the door for her. But Gilchrist, at this moment, was an enemy, the last person in the world in whom her mistress would confide; Gilchrist, who had never believed in it, had refused to see the likeness, or to encourage any delusion. She was blind to the woman's imploring looks, her breathless "Oh, mem!" which was more than any question, and brushed past her with the same iron rigidity of pose, which had taken all softness from her natural angularity. She walked straight into her bedroom, where she took off her bonnet before the glass, without awaiting Gilchrist's ministrations, nay, putting them aside with a quick impatient gesture. Then she went to her sitting-room, and drew her chair into her favourite position near the window, and took up the paper and began to read it with every appearance of intense interest. She had read it through every word, as is the practice of lonely ladies, before she went out : and she was profoundly conscious now of Gilchrist following her about, hovering behind her, and more anxious than words can say. Miss Bethune was an hour or more occupied about that newspaper, of which she did not see a single word, and then she rose suddenly to her feet.

"I cannot do it—I cannot do it!" she cried. "The woman has no claim on me. Most likely she's nothing but a fool, that has spoilt everything for herself, and more. Maybe it will not be good for Dora. But I cannot do it—I cannot do it.

It's too strong for me. Whatever comes of it, she must see her child—she must see her child before she passes away and is no more seen. And oh, I wish—I wish that it was not her, but me!"

CHAPTER XVI.

DORA passed the long evening of that day in her father's room. It was one of those days in which the sun seems to refuse to set, the daylight to depart. It rolled out in afternoon sunshine, prolonged as it seemed for half a year's time, showing no inclination to wane. When the sun at last went down, there ensued a long interval of day without it, and slowly, slowly, the shades of twilight came on. Mr. Mannering had been very quiet all the afternoon. He had sat brooding, unwilling to speak. The big book came back with Mr. Fiddler's compliments, and was replaced upon his table, where he sat sometimes turning over the pages, not reading, doing nothing. There are few things more terrible to a looker-on than this silence, this self-absorption, taking no

notice of anything outside of him, of a convalescent. The attitude of despondency, the bowed
head, the curved shoulders, are bad enough in
themselves : but nothing is so dreadful as the
silence, the preoccupation with nothing, the eyes
fixed on a page which is not read, or a horizon in
which nothing is visible. Dora sat by him with
a book, too, in which she was interested, which is
perhaps the easiest way of bearing this ; but the
book ended before the afternoon did, and then
she had nothing to do but to watch him and wonder what he was thinking of—whether his mind
was roving over lands unknown to her, whether
it was about the Museum he was thinking, or the
doctor's orders, or the bills, two or three of which
had by misadventure fallen into his hands. What
was it ? He remained in the same attitude, quite
still and steady, not moving a finger. Sometimes
she hoped he might have fallen asleep; sometimes
she addressed to him a faltering question, to which

he answered Yes or No. He was not impatient when she spoke to him. He replied to her in monosyllables, which are almost worse than silence. And Dora durst not protest, could not upbraid him with that dreadful silence, as an older person might have done. "Oh, father, talk to me a little!" she once cried in her despair; but he said gently that he had nothing to talk about, and silenced the girl. He had taken the various meals and refreshments that were ordered for him, when they came, with something that was half a smile and half a look of disgust; and this was the final exasperation to Dora.

"Oh, father! when you know that you must take it—that it is the only way of getting well again."

"I am taking it," he said, with that twist of the lip at every spoonful which betrayed how distasteful it was.

This is hard to bear for the most experienced

of nurses, and what should it be for a girl of sixteen ?   She clasped her hands together in her impatience to keep herself down.   And then there
came a knock at the door, and Gilchrist appeared,
begging that Miss Dora would put on her hat and
go out for a walk with Miss Bethune.

" I'll come and sit with my work in a corner
and be there if he wants anything."

Mr. Mannering did not seem to take any notice,
but he heard the whisper at the door.

" There is no occasion for any one sitting
with me.   I am quite able to ring if I want
anything."

"But, father, I don't want to go out," said
Dora.

" I want you to go out," he said peremptorily.
" It is not proper that you should be shut up here
all day."

" Let me light the candles, then, father ? "

" I don't want any candles.   I am not doing

anything. There is plenty of light for what I want."

Oh, what despair it was to have to do with a man who would not be shaken, who would take his own way and no other! If he would but have read a novel, as Dora did—if he would but return to the study of his big book, which was the custom of his life. Dora felt that it was almost wicked to leave him : but what could she do, while he sat there absorbed in his thoughts, which she could not even divine what they were about?

To go out into the cool evening was a relief to her poor little exasperated temper and troubled mind. The air was sweet and fresh, even in Bloomsbury ; the trees waved and rustled softly against the blue sky ; there was a young moon somewhere, a white speck in the blue, though the light of day was not yet gone ; the voices were softened and almost musical in the evening air, and it was so good to be out of doors, to be

removed from the close controlling atmosphere
of unaccustomed trouble. "Out of sight, out of
mind," people say. It was very far from being
that ; on the contrary, it was but the natural impatience, the mere contrariety, that had made the
girl ready to cry with a sense of the intolerable
which now was softened and subdued, allowing
love and pity to come back. She could talk of
nothing but her father as she went along the
street.

"Do you think he looks any better, Miss
Bethune ? Do you think he will soon be able
to get out ? Do you think the doctor will let
him return soon to the Museum ? He loves
the Museum better than anything. He would
have more chance to get well if he might go
back."

"All that must be decided by time, Dora—
time and the doctor, who, though we scoff at him
sometimes, knows better, after all, than you or me.

But I want you to think a little of the poor lady you are going to see."

"What am I going to see? Oh, that lady? I don't know if father will wish me to see her. Oh, I did not know what it was you wanted of me. I cannot go against father, Miss Bethune, when he is ill and does not know."

"You will just trust to another than your father for once in your life, Dora. If you think I am not a friend to your father, and one that would consider him in all things ——"

The girl walked on silently, reluctantly, for some time without speaking, with sometimes a half pause, as if she would have turned back. Then she answered in a low voice, still not very willingly: " I know you are a friend ".

"You do not put much heart in it," said Miss Bethune, with a laugh. The most magnanimous person, when conscious of having been very help-ful and a truly good friend at his or her personal expense to another, may be pardoned a sense of humour, partially bitter, in the grudging acknowledgment of ignorance. Then she added more gravely : " When your father knows—and he shall know in time—where I am taking you, he will approve ; whatever his feelings may be, he will tell you it was right and your duty : of that I am as sure as that I am living, Dora."

" Because she is my aunt ? An aunt is not such a very tender relation, Miss Bethune. In books they are often very cold comforters, not kind to girls that are poor. I suppose," said Dora, after a little pause, "that I would be called poor ? "

"You are just nothing, you foolish little thing! You have no character of your own; you are your father's daughter, and no more."

" I don't wish to be anything more," cried Dora, with her foolish young head held high.

" And this poor woman," said Miss Bethune,

exasperated, "will not live long enough to be a friend to any one—so you need not be afraid either of her being too tender or unkind. She has come back, poor thing, after long years spent out of her own country, to die."

"To die?" the girl echoed in a horrified tone.

"Just that, and nothing less or more."

Dora walked on by Miss Bethune's side for some time in silence. There was a long, very long walk through the streets before they reached the coolness and freshness of the Park. She said nothing for a long time, until they had arrived at the Serpentine, which—veiled in shadows and mists of night, with the stars reflected in it, and the big buildings in the distance standing up solemnly, half seen, yet with gleams of lamps and light all over them, beyond, and apparently among the trees—has a sort of splendour and reality, like a great natural river flowing between its banks. She paused there for a moment, and asked, with a quick drawing of her breath : " Is it some one—who is dying—that you are taking me to see ? "

" Yes, Dora ; and next to your father, your nearest relation in the world."

" I thought at one time that he was going to die, Miss Bethune."

" So did we all, Dora."

" And I was very much afraid—oh, not only heartbroken, but afraid. I thought he would suffer so, in himself," she said very low, " and to leave me."

" They do not," said Miss Bethune with great solemnity, as if not of any individual, but of a mysterious class of people. " They are delivered; anxious though they may have been, they are anxious no more ; though their hearts would have broken to part with you a little while before, it is no longer so ; they are delivered. It's a very solemn thing," she went on, with something like a

sob in her voice; "but it's comforting, at least to
the like of me. Their spirits are changed, they
are separated; there are other things before them
greater than what they leave behind."

"Oh," cried the girl, "I should not like to
think of that: if father had ceased to think of me
even before ——"

"It is comforting to me," said Miss Bethune,
"because I am of those that are going, and you,
Dora, are of those that are staying. I'm glad to
think that the silver chain will be loosed and the
golden bowl broken—all the links that bind us to
the earth, and all the cares about what is to
happen after."

"Have you cares about what is to happen
after?" cried Dora. "Father has, for he has me;
but you, Miss Bethune?"

Dora never forgot, or thought she would
never forget, the look that was cast upon her.
"And I," said Miss Bethune, "have not even

you, have nobody belonging to me. Well," she said, going on with a heavy long-drawn breath, "it looks as if it were true."

This was the girl's first discovery of what youth is generally so long in finding out, that in her heedlessness and unconscious conviction that what related to herself was the most important in the world, and what befel an elderly neighbour of so much less consequence, she had done, or at least said, a cruel thing. But she did not know how to mend matters, and so went on by her friend's side dumb, confusedly trying to enter into, now that it was too late, the sombre complications of another's thought. Nothing more was said till they were close to the great hotel, which shone out with its many windows luminous upon the soft background of the night. Then Miss Bethune put her hand almost harshly upon Dora's arm.

"You will remember, Dora," she said, "that

the person, we are going to see is a dying person, and in all the world it is agreed that where a dying person is, he or she is the chief person, and to be considered above all. It is, maybe, a superstition, but it is so allowed. Their wants and their wishes go before all; and the queen herself, if she were coming into that chamber, would bow to it like all the rest : and so must you. It is, perhaps, not quite sincere, for why should a woman be more thought of because she is going to die? That is not a quality, you will say : but yet it's a superstition, and approved of by all the civilised world."

"Oh, Miss Bethune," cried Dora, "I know that I deserve that you should say this to me : but yet ——"

Her companion made no reply, but led the way up the great stairs.

The room was not so dark as before, though it was night ; a number of candles were shining

in the farther corner near the bed, and the pale
face on the pillow, the nostrils dark and widely
opened with the panting breath, was in full light,
turned towards the door.   A nurse in her white
apron and cap was near the bed, beside a maid
whose anxious face was strangely contrasted with
the calm of the professional person.   These ac-
cessories Dora's quick glance took in at once,
while yet her attention was absorbed in the cen-
tral figure, which she needed no further explana-
tion to perceive had at once become the first
object, the chief interest, to all near her.   Dying!
It was more than mere reigning, more than being
great.   To think that where she lay, there she was
going fast away into the most august presence,
to the deepest wonders!   Dora held her breath
with awe.   She never, save when her father was
swimming for his life, and her thoughts were con-
centrated on the struggle with all the force of
personal passion, as if it were she herself who was

fighting against death, had seen any such sight
before.

"Is it Dora?" cried the patient. "Dora!
Oh, my child, my child, have you come at last?"

And then Dora found arms round her clutching her close, and felt with a strange awe, not un-
mingled with terror, the wild beating of a feverish
heart, and the panting of a laborious breath.
The wan face was pressed against hers. She felt
herself held for a moment with extraordinary
force, and kisses, tears, and always the beat of
that troubled breathing, upon her cheek. Then
the grasp relaxed reluctantly, because the sufferer
could do no more.

"Oh, gently, gently; do not wear yourself
out. She is not going away. She has come to
stay with you," a soothing voice said.

"That's all I want—all I want in this world—
what I came for," gave forth the panting lips.

Dora's impulse was to cry, "No, no!" to

rise up from her knees, upon which she had fallen unconsciously by the sick bed, to withdraw from it, and if possible get away altogether, terrified of that close vicinity : but partly what Miss Bethune had said, and partly natural feeling, the instinct of humanity, kept her in spite of herself where she was. The poor lady lay with her face intent upon Dora, stroking her hair and her forehead with those hot thin hands, beaming upon her with that ineffable smile which is the prerogative of the dying.

" Oh, my little girl," she said,—" my only one, my only one ! Twelve years it is—twelve long years—and all the time thinking of this ! When I've been ill,—and I've been very ill, Miller will tell you,—I've kept up, I've forced myself to be better for this—for this ! "

" You will wear yourself out, ma'am," said the nurse. " You must not talk, you must be quiet, or I shall have to send the young lady away."

" No, no!" cried the dying woman, again clutching Dora with fevered arms. " For what must I be quiet ?—to live a little longer ? I only want to live while she's here. I only want it as long as I can see her—Dora, you'll stay with me, you'll stay with your poor—poor ——"

" She shall stay as long as you want her : but for God's sake think of something else, woman— think of where you're going !" cried Miss Bethune harshly over Dora's head.

They disposed of her at their ease, talking over her head, bandying her about—she who was mistress of her own actions, who had never been made to stay where she did not wish to stay, or to go where she did not care to go. But Dora was silent even in the rebellion of her spirit. There was a something more strong than herself, which kept her there on her knees in the middle of the circle—all, as · Miss Bethune had said, attending on the one who was dying, the one who was of the first interest, to whom even the queen would bow and defer if she were to come in here. Dora did not know what to say to a person in such a position. She approved, yet was angry that Miss Bethune should bid the poor lady think where she was going. She was frightened and excited, not knowing what dreadful change might take place, what alteration, before her very eyes. Her heart began to beat wildly against her breast; pity was in it, but fear too, which is masterful and obliterates other emotions: yet even that was kept in check by the overwhelming influence, the fascination of the chamber of death.

Then there was a pause; and Dora, still on her knees by the side of the bed, met as best she could the light which dazzled her, which enveloped her in a kind of pale flame, from the eyes preternaturally bright that were fixed upon her face, and listened, as to a kind of strange lullaby, to the broken words of fondness, a murmur of fond

names, of half sentences, and monosyllables, in the
silence of the hushed room.   This seemed to last
for a long time.   She was conscious of people
passing with hushed steps behind her, looking
over her head, a man's low voice, the whisper of
the nurses, a movement of the lights ; but always
that transfigured face, all made of whiteness,
luminous, the hot breath coming and going, the
hands about her face, the murmur of words.   The
girl was cramped with her attitude for a time, and
then the cramp went away, and her body became
numb, keeping its position like a mechanical
thing, while her mind too was lulled into a curious
sense of torpor, yet spectatorship.   This lasted
she did not know how long.   She ceased to be
aware of what was being said to her.   Her own
name, " Dora," over and over again repeated, and
strange words, that came back to her afterwards,
went on in a faltering stream.   Hours might have
passed for anything she knew, when at last she

was raised, scarcely capable of feeling anything, and put into a chair by the bedside. She became dimly conscious that the brilliant eyes that had been gazing at her so long were being veiled as with sleep, but they opened again suddenly as she was removed, and were fixed upon her with an anguish of entreaty. " Dora, my child,—my child ! Don't take her away ! "

" She is going to sit by you here," said a voice, which could only be a doctor's voice, " here by your bedside. It is easier for her. She is not going away."

Then the ineffable smile came back. The two thin hands enveloped Dora's wrist, holding her hand close between them ; and again there came a wonderful interval—the dark room, the little stars of lights, the soft movements of the attendants gradually fixing themselves like a picture on Dora's mind. Miss Bethune was behind in the dark, sitting bolt upright against the wall, and never moving. Shadowed by the curtains at the foot of the bed was some one with a white and anxious face, whom Dora had only seen in the cheerful light, and could scarcely identify as Harry Gordon. A doctor and the white-capped nurse were in front, the maid crying behind. It seemed to go on again and last for hours this strange scene—until there suddenly arose a little commotion and movement about the bed, Dora could not tell why. Her hand was liberated ; the other figures came between her and the wan face on the pillow, and she found herself suddenly, swiftly swept away. She neither made any resistance nor yet moved of her own will, and scarcely knew what was happening until she felt the fresh night air on her face, and found herself in a carriage, with Harry Gordon's face, very grave and white, at the window.

" You will come to me in the morning and let

me know the arrangements," Miss Bethune said,
in a low voice.

"Yes, I will come ; and thank you, thank you
a thousand times for bringing her," he said.

They all talked of Dora as if she were a
thing, as if she had nothing to do with herself.
Her mind was roused by the motion, by the air
blowing in her face. "What has happened?
What has happened?" she asked as they drove
away.

"Will she be up yonder already, beyond that
shining sky?   Will she know as she is known?
Will she be satisfied with His likeness, and be
like Him, seeing Him as He is?" said Miss
Bethune, looking up at the stars, with her eyes
full of big tears.

"Oh, tell me," cried Dora, "what has
happened?" with a sob of excitement; for
whether she was sorry, or only awe-stricken,
she did not know.

"Just everything has happened that can happen to a woman here. She has got safe away out of it all; and there are few, few at my time of life, that would not be thankful to be like her—out of it all: though it may be a great thought to go."

"Do you mean that the lady is dead?" Dora asked in a voice of awe.

"She is dead, as we say; and content, having had her heart's desire."

"Was that me?" cried Dora, humbled by a great wonder. "Me? Why should she have wanted me so much as that, and not to let me go?"

"Oh, child, I know no more than you, and yet I know well, well! Because she was your mother, and you were all she had in the world."

"My mother's sister," said Dora, with childish sternness; "and," she added after a moment, "not my father's friend."

"Oh, hard life and hard judgment!" cried Miss Bethune. "Your mother's own self, a poor martyr : except that at the last she has had, what not every woman has, for a little moment, her heart's desire!"

CHAPTER XVII.

Young Gordon went into Miss Bethune's sitting-room next morning so early that she was still at breakfast, lingering over her second cup of tea. His eyes had the look of eyes which had not slept, and that air of mingled fatigue and excitement which shows that a great crisis which had just come was about his whole person. His energetic young limbs were languid with it. He threw himself into a chair, as if even that support and repose were comfortable, and an ease to his whole being.

"She rallied for a moment after you were gone," he said in a low voice, not looking at his companion, "but not enough to notice anything. The doctor said there was no pain or suffering— if he knows anything about it."

(69)

"Ay, if he knows," Miss Bethune said.

"And so she is gone," said the young man with a deep sigh. He struggled for a moment with his voice, which went from him in the sudden access of sorrow. After a minute he resumed: "She's gone, and my occupation, all my reasons for living, seem to be gone too. I know no more what is going to happen. I was her son yesterday, and did everything for her; now I don't know what I am. I am nobody, with scarcely the right even to be there."

"What do you mean? Everybody must know what you have been to her, and her to you, all your life."

The young man was leaning forward in his chair bent almost double, with his eyes fixed on the floor. "Yes," he said, "I never understood it before: but I know now what it is to have no rightful place, to have been only a dependent on their` kindness. When my guardian died I did not feel it, because she was still there to think of me, and I was her representative in everything; but now the solicitor has taken the command, and makes me see I am nobody. It is not for the money," the young man said, with a wave of his hand. " Let that go however she wished. God knows I would never complain. But I might have been allowed to do something for her, to manage things for her as I have done—oh, almost ever since I can remember." He looked up with a pale and troubled smile, wistful for sympathy. " I feel as if I had been cut adrift," he said.

" My poor boy! But she must have provided for you, fulfilled the expectations ——"

" Don't say that!" he cried quickly. " There were no expectations. I can truly say I never thought upon the subject—never!—until we came here to London. Then it was forced upon me that I was good for nothing, did not know how

to make my living.   It was almost amusing at
first, I was so unused to it ; but not now.   I am
afraid I am quite useless," he added, with again
a piteous smile.   " I am in the state of the poor
fellow in the Bible.   ' I can't dig, and to beg I
am ashamed.'   I don't know," he cried, " why I
should trouble you with all this.   But you said
I was to come to you in the morning, and I feel
I can speak to you.   That's about all the expla-
nation there is."

" It's the voice of nature," cried Miss Bethune
quickly, an eager flush covering her face.   " Don't
you know, don't you feel, that there is nobody
but me you could come to?—that you are sure of
me whoever fails you—that there's a sympathy,
and more than a sympathy ? Oh, my boy, I will
be to you all, and more than all !"

She was so overcome with her own emotion
that she could not get out another word.

A flush came also upon Harry Gordon's pale

face, a look abashed and full of wonder. He felt
that this lady, whom he liked and respected, went
so much too far, so much farther than there was
any justification for doing. He was troubled
instinctively for her, that she should be so impulsive, so strangely affected. He shook his head.
" Don't think me ungrateful," he cried. "Indeed,
I don't know if you mean all that your words
seem to mean—as how should you indeed, and I
only a stranger to you? But, dear Miss Bethune,
that can never be again. It is bad enough, as I
find out, to have had no real tie to her, my dear
lady that's gone—and to feel that everybody must
think my grief for my poor aunt is partly disappointment because she has not provided for me.
But no such link could be forged again. I was a
child when that was made. It was natural ; they
settled things for me as they pleased, and I knew
nothing but that I was very happy there, and
loved them, and they me. But now I am a man,

and must stand for myself. Don't think me un-
gracious. It's impossible but that a man with full
use of his limbs must be able to earn his bread.
It's only going back to South America, if the
worst comes to the worst, where everybody knows
me," he said.

Miss Bethune's countenance had been like a
drama while young Gordon made this long speech,
most of which was uttered with little breaks and
pauses, without looking at her, in the same attitude, with his eyes on the ground. Yet he
looked up once or twice with that flitting sad
smile, and an air of begging pardon for anything
he said which might wound her. Trouble, and
almost shame, and swift contradiction, and anger,
and sympathy, and tender pity, and a kind of
admiration, all went over her face in waves. She
was wounded by what he said, and disappointed,
and yet approved. Could there be all these things
in the hard lines of a middle-aged face? And yet

there were all, and more. She recovered herself quickly as he came to an end, and with her usual voice replied :—

" We must not be so hasty to begin with. It is more than likely that the poor lady has made the position clear in her will. We must not jump to the conclusion that things are not explained in that and set right ; it would be a slur upon her memory even to think that it would not be so."

" There must be no slur on her memory," said young Gordon quickly ; " but I am almost sure that it will not be so. She told me repeatedly that I was not to blame her—as if it were likely I should blame her !"

" She would deserve blame," cried Miss Bethune quickly, " if after all that has passed she should leave you with no provision, no acknowledgment ——"

He put up his hand to stop her.

"Not a word of that! What I wanted was to keep my place until after---until all was done for her. I am a mere baby," he cried, dashing away the tears from his eyes. " It was that solicitor coming in to take charge of everything, to lock up everything, to give all the orders, that was more than I could bear."

She did not trust herself to say anything, but laid her hand upon his arm. And the poor young fellow was at the end of his forces, worn out bodily with anxiety and want of sleep, and mentally by grief and the conflict of emotions. He bent down his face upon her hand, kissing it with a kind of passion, and burst out, leaning his head upon her arm, into a storm of tears, that broke from him against his will. Miss Bethune put her other hand upon his bowed head ; her face quivered with the yearning of her whole life. " Oh, God, is he my bairn ?—Oh, God, that he were my bairn ! " she cried.

But nobody would have guessed what this crisis had been who saw them a little after, as Dora saw them, who came into the room pale too with the unusual vigil of the previous night, but full of an indignant something which she had to say. " Miss Bethune," she cried, almost before she had closed the door, "do you know what Gilchrist told father about last night?—that I was tired when I came in, and had a headache, and she had put me to bed! And now I have to tell lies too, to say I am better, and to agree when he thanks Gilchrist for her care, and says it was the best thing for me. Oh, what a horrible thing it is to tell lies! To hide things from him, and invent excuses, and cheat him—cheat him with stories that are not true ! "

Her hair waved behind her, half curling, crisp, inspired by indignation : her slim figure seemed to expand and grow, her eyes shone. Miss Bethune had certainly not gained anything by the

deceptions, which were very innocent ones after
all, practised upon Mr. Mannering : but she had
to bear the brunt of this shock with what composure she might.   She laughed a little, half glad
to shake off the fumes of deeper emotion in
this new incident.   " As soon as he is stronger
you shall explain everything to him, Dora,"
she said.   " When the body is weak the mind
should not be vexed more than is possible with
perplexing things or petty cares.   But as soon as
he is better ——"

   " And now," cried Dora, flinging back her hair,
all crisped, and almost scintillating, with anger and
distress, her eyes filled with tears, " here comes
the doctor now—far, far worse than any bills or
any perplexities, and tells him straight out that he
must ask for a year's holiday and go away, first
for the rest of the summer, and then for the
winter, as father says, to one of those places where
all the fools go !—father, whose life is in the

Museum, who cares for nothing else, who can't bear
to go away! Oh!" cried Dora, stamping her foot,
"to think I should be made to lie, to keep little,
little things from him—contemptible things! and
that then the doctor should come straight upstairs
and without any preface, without any apology,
blurt out that!"

"The doctor must have thought, Dora, it
was better for him to know.   He says all will go
well, he will get quite strong, and be able to work
in the Museum to his heart's content, if only he
will do this now."

"If only he will do this!   If only he will invent a lot of money, father says, which we haven't
got.   And how is the money to be invented?   It
is like telling poor Mrs. Hesketh not to walk, but
to go out in a carriage every day.   Perhaps that
would make her quite well, poor thing.   It would
make the beggar at the corner quite well if he
had turtle soup and champagne like father.   And

we must stop even the turtle soup and the champagne. He will not have them; they make him angry now that he has come to himself. Cannot you see, Miss Bethune," cried Dora with youthful superiority, as if such a thought could never have occurred to her friend, "that we can only do things which we can do—that there are some things that are impossible? Oh!" she said suddenly, perceiving for the first time young Gordon with a start of annoyance and surprise. "I did not know," cried Dora, "that I was discussing our affairs before a gentleman who can't take any interest in them."

"Dora, is that all you have to say to one that shared our watch last night—that has just come, as it were, from her that is gone? Have you no thought of that poor lady, and what took place so lately? Oh, my dear, have a softer heart."

"Miss Bethune," said Dora with dignity, "I

am very sorry for the poor lady of last night. I was a little angry because I was made to deceive father, but my heart was not hard. I was very sorry. But how can I go on thinking about her when I have father to think of? I could not be fond of her, could I? I did not know her—I never saw her but once before. If she was my mother's sister, she was—she confessed it herself—father's enemy. I must—I must be on father's side," cried Dora. "I have had no one else all my life."

Miss Bethune and her visitor looked at each other,—he with a strange painful smile, she with tears in her eyes. "It is just the common way," she said,—"just the common way! You look over the one that loves you, and you heap love upon the one that loves you not."

"It cannot be the common way," said Gordon, "for the circumstances are not common. It is because of strange things, and relations that are not natural. I had no right to that love you speak of, and Dora had. But I have got all the advantages of it for many a year. There is no injustice if she who has the natural right to it gets it now."

"Oh, my poor boy," cried Miss Bethune, "you argue well, but you know better in your heart."

"I have not a grudge in my heart," he exclaimed, "not one, nor a complaint. Oh, believe me!—except to be put away as if I were nobody, just at this moment when there was still something to do for her," he said, after a pause.

Dora looked from one to the other, half wondering, half impatient. "You are talking of Mr. Gordon's business now," she said; "and I have nothing to do with that, any more than he has to do with mine. I had better go back to father, Miss Bethune, if you will tell Dr. Roland that he is cruel—that he ought to have waited till father was stronger—that it was wicked—wicked —to go and pour out all that upon him without any preparation, when even I was out of the way."

"Indeed, I think there is reason in what you say, Dora," said Miss Bethune, as the girl went away.

"It will not matter," said Gordon, after the door was closed. "That is one thing to be glad of, there will be no more want of money. Now," he said, rising, "I must go back again. It has been a relief to come and tell you everything, but now it seems as if I had a hunger to go back : and yet it is strange to go back. It is strange to walk about the streets and to know that I have nobody to go home to, that she is far away, and unmoved by anything that can happen to me." He paused a moment, and added, with that low laugh which is the alternative of tears : " Not to say that there

is no home to go back to, nothing but a room in a
hotel which I must get out of as soon as possible,
and nobody belonging to me, or that I belong
to.   It is so difficult to get accustomed to the
idea."

Miss Bethune gave a low cry.   It was inarticu-
late, but she could not restrain it.   She put out
both her hands, then drew them back again ; and
after he had gone away, she went on pacing up and
down the room, making this involuntary movement,
murmuring that outcry, which was not even a
word, to herself.   She put out her hands, sometimes her arms, then brought them back and
pressed them to the heart which seemed to be
bursting from her breast.   "Oh, if it might still
be that he were mine !   Oh, if I might believe it
(as I do—I do !) and take him to me whether or
no !"   Her thoughts shaped themselves as their
self-repression gave way to that uncontrollable
tide.   "Oh, well might he say that it was not the

common way! the woman that had been a mother
to him, thinking no more of him the moment her
own comes in! And might I be like that? If
I took him to my heart, that I think must be
mine, and then the other, the true one—that
would know nothing of me! And he, what does
he know of me?—what does he think of me?—
an old fool that puts out my arms to him without rhyme or reason. But then it's to me he
comes when he's in trouble; he comes to me, he
leans his head on me, just by instinct, by nature.
And nature cries out in me here." She put her
hands once more with unconscious dramatic
action to her heart. " Nature cries out—nature
cries out!"

Unconsciously she said these words aloud, and
herself startled by the sound of her own voice,
looked up suddenly, to see Gilchrist, who had just
come into the room, standing gazing at her with
an expression of pity and condemnation which

drove her mistress frantic. Miss Bethune coloured high. She stopped in a moment her agitated walk, and placed herself in a chair with an air of hauteur and loftiness difficult to describe. " Well," she said, " were you wanting anything?" as if the excellent and respectable person standing before her had been, as Gilchrist herself said afterwards, "the scum of the earth ".

" No' much, mem," said Gilchrist ; "only to know if you were"—poor Gilchrist was so frightened by her mistress's aspect that she invented reasons which had no sound of truth in them—" going out this morning, or wanting your seam or the stocking you were knitting."

" Did you think I had all at once become doited, and did not know what I wanted?" asked Miss Bethune sternly.

Gilchrist made no reply, but dropped her guilty head.

"To think," cried the lady, "that I cannot have a visitor in the morning—a common visitor like those that come and go about every idle person,—nor take a thought into my mind, nor say a word even to myself, but in comes an intrusive serving-woman to worm out of me, with her frightened looks and her peety and her compassion, what it's all about! Lord! if it were any other than a woman that's been about me twenty years, and had just got herself in to be a habit and a custom, that would dare to come with her soft looks peetying me!"

Having come to a climax, voice and feeling together, in those words, Miss Bethune suddenly burst into the tempest of tears which all this time had been gathering and growing beyond any power of hers to restrain them.

"Oh, my dear leddy, my dear leddy!" Gilchrist said; then, gradually drawing nearer, took her

mistress's head upon her ample bosom till the fit
was over.

When Miss Bethune had calmed herself again,
she pushed the maid away.

"I'll have no communication with you," she
said. "You're a good enough servant, you're not
an ill woman ; but as for real sympathy or support
in what is most dear, it's no' you that will give
them to any person. I'm neither wanting to go
out nor to take my seam. I will maybe read a
book to quiet myself down, but I'm not meaning
to hold any communication with you."

"Oh, mem!" said Gilchrist, in appeal : but
she was not deeply cast down. "If it was about
the young gentleman," she added, after a moment,
"I just think he is as nice a young gentleman as
the world contains."

"Did I not tell you so?" cried the mistress
in triumph. "And like the gracious blood he's
come of," she said, rising to her feet again, as if

she were waving a flag of victory. Then she sat down abruptly, and opened upside down the book she had taken from the table. "But I'll hold no communication with you on that subject," she said.

CHAPTER XVIII.

Mr. Mannering had got into his sitting-room the next day, as the first change for which he was able in his convalescent state. The doctor's decree, that he must give up work for a year, and spend the winter abroad, had been fulminated forth upon him in the manner described by Dora, as a means of rousing him from the lethargy into which he was falling. After Dr. Roland had refused to permit of his speedy return to the Museum, he had become indifferent to everything except the expenses, concerning which he was now on the most jealous watch, declining to taste the dainties that were brought to him. "I cannot afford it," was his constant cry. He had ceased to desire to get up, to dress, to read, which, in preparation, as he hoped, for going out again, he had been at first so eager to do. Then the doctor had delivered his full broadside. "You may think what you like of me, Mannering; of course, it's in your power to defy me and die. You can if you like, and nobody can stop you: but if you care for anything in this world,—for that child who has no protector but you,"—here the doctor made a pause full of force, and fixed the patient with his eyes,—"you will dismiss all other considerations, and make up your mind to do what will make you well again, without any more nonsense. You must do it, and nothing less will do."

"Tell the beggar round the corner to go to Italy for the winter," said the invalid; "he'll manage it better than I. A man can beg anywhere, he carries his profession about with him. That's, I suppose, what you mean me to do."

" I don't care what you do," cried Dr. Roland,
" as long as you do what I say."

Mr. Mannering was so indignant, so angry,
so roused and excited, that he walked into his
sitting-room that afternoon breathing fire and
flame. " I shall return to the Museum next
week," he said. " Let them do what they please,
Dora. Italy! And what better is Italy than
England, I should like to know? A blazing hot,
deadly cold, impudently beautiful country. No
repose in it, always in extremes like a scene in a
theatre, or else like chill desolation, misery, and
death. I'll not hear a word of Italy. The South
of France is worse; all the exaggerations of the
other, and a volcano underneath. He may rave
till he burst, I will not go. The Museum is the
place for me—or the grave, which might be better
still."

" Would you take me there with you, father?"
said Dora.

"Child!" He said this word in such a tone that no capitals in the world could give any idea of it ; and then that brought him to a pause, and increased the force of the hot stimulant that already was working in his veins. "But we have no money," he cried,—"no money—no money! Do you understand that ? I have been a fool. I have been going on spending everything I had. I never expected a long illness, doctors and nurses, and all those idiotic luxuries. I can eat a chop— do you hear, Dora?—a chop, the cheapest you can get. I can live on dry bread. But get into debt I will not—not for you and all your doctors. There's that Fiddler and his odious book—three pounds ten—what for ? For a piece of vanity, to say I had the 1490 edition : not even to say it, for who cares except some of the men at the Museum ? What does Roland understand about the 1490 edition ? He probably thinks the latest edition is always the best. And I—a

confounded fool—throwing away my money—
your money, my poor child!—for I can't take
you with me, Dora, as you say. God forbid—
God forbid!"

"Well, father," said Dora, who had gone
through many questions with herself since the
conversation in Miss Bethune's room, "suppose
we were to try and think how it is to be done.
No doubt, as he is the doctor, however we rebel,
he will make us do it at the last."

"How can he make us do it? He cannot put
money in my pocket, he cannot coin money, however much he would like it; and if he could, I
suppose he would keep it for himself."

"I am not so sure of that, father."

"I am sure of this, that he ought to, if he is
not a fool. Every man ought to who has a spark
of sense in him. I have not done it, and you see
what happens. Roland may be a great idiot, but
not so great an idiot as I."

"Oh, father, what is the use of talking like this? Let us try and think how we are to do it," Dora cried.

His renewed outcry that he could not do it, that it was not a thing to be thought of for a moment, was stopped by a knock at the door, at which, when Dora, after vainly bidding the unknown applicant come in, opened it, there appeared an old gentleman, utterly unknown to both, and whose appearance was extremely disturbing to the invalid newly issued from his sick room, and the girl who still felt herself his nurse and protector.

"I hope I do not come at a bad moment," the stranger said. "I took the opportunity of an open door to come straight up without having myself announced. I trust I may be pardoned for the liberty. Mr. Mannering, you do not recollect me, but I have seen you before. I am Mr. Templar, of Gray's Inn. I have something of importance to say to you, which will, I trust, excuse my intrusion."

"Oh," cried Dora. "I am sure you cannot know that my father has been very ill. He is out of his room for the first time to-day."

The old gentleman said that he was very sorry, and then that he was very glad. "That means in a fair way of recovery," he said. "I don't know," he added, addressing Mannering, who was pondering over him with a somewhat sombre countenance, "whether I may speak to you about my business, Mr. Mannering, at such an early date : but I am almost forced to do so by my orders : and whether you would rather hear my commission in presence of this young lady or not."

"Where is it we have met?" Mannering said, with a more and more gloomy look.

"I will tell you afterwards, if you will hear me in the first place. I come to announce to you, Mr. Mannering, the death of a client of mine, who has left a very considerable fortune to your daughter, Dora Mannering—this young lady, I presume : and with it a prayer that the young lady, to whom she leaves everything, may be permitted to—may, with your consent ——"

"Oh," cried Dora, " I know! It is the poor lady from South America!" And then she became silent and grew red. "Father, I have hid something from you," she said, faltering. "I have seen a lady, forgive me, who was your enemy. She said you would never forgive her. Oh, how one's sins find one out! It was not my fault that I went, and I thought you would never know. She was mamma's sister, father."

"She was—who?" Mr. Mannering rose from his chair. He had been pale before, he became now livid, yellow, his thin cheek-bones standing out, his hollow eyes with a glow in them, his mouth drawn in. He towered over the two people beside him—Dora frightened and protesting, the visitor very calm and observant—looking twice his height in his extreme leanness and gauntness. " Who—who was it? Who? " His whole face asked the question.   He stood a moment tottering, then dropped back in complete exhaustion into his chair.

" Father," cried Dora, " I did not know who she was.   She was very ill and wanted me.   It was she who used to send me those things.   Miss Bethune took me, it was only once, and I—I was there when she died."   The recollection choked her voice, and made her tremble.   " Father, she said you would not forgive her, that you were never to be told ; but I could not believe," cried Dora, " that there was any one, ill or sorry, and very, very weak, and in trouble, whom you would not forgive."

Mr. Mannering sat gazing at his child, with his eyes burning in their sockets.   At these words he covered his face with his hands.   And there was silence, save for a sob of excitement from Dora, excitement so long repressed that it burst forth now with all the greater force.   The visitor, for some time, did not say a word.   Then suddenly he put forth his hand and touched the elbow which rested like a sharp point on the table. He said softly : "It was the lady you imagine. She is dead.   She has led a life of suffering and trouble.   She has neither been well nor happy. Her one wish was to see her child before she died.   When she was left free, as happened by death some time ago, she came to England for that purpose.   I can't tell you how much or how little the friends knew, who helped her.   They thought it, I believe, a family quarrel."

Mr. Mannering uncovered his ghastly countenance.   "It is better they should continue to think so."

"That is as you please.   For my own part, I think the child at least should know.   The request, the prayer that was made on her death-bed in all humility, was that Dora should follow her remains to the grave."

" To what good ? " he cried, " to what good ? "

" To no good.   Have you forgotten her, that you ask that ?   I told her, if she had asked to see you, to get your forgiveness ——"

" Silence ! " cried Mr. Mannering, lifting his thin hand as if with a threat.

" But she had not courage.   She wanted only, she said, her own flesh and blood to stand by her grave."

Mannering made again a gesture with his hand, but no reply.

" She has left everything of which she died possessed—a considerable, I may say a large fortune—to her only child."

" I refuse her fortune ! " cried Mannering, bringing down his clenched hand on the table with a feverish force that made the room ring.

"You will not be so pitiless," said the
visitor; "you will not pursue an unfortunate
woman, who never in her unhappy life meant
any harm."

"In her unhappy life!—in her pursuit of a
happy life at any cost, that is what you mean."

"I will not argue. She is dead. Say she
was thoughtless, fickle. I can't tell. She did
only what she was justified in doing. She meant
no harm."

"I will allow no one," cried Mr. Mannering,
"to discuss the question with me. Your client, I
understand, is dead,—it was proper, perhaps, that
I should know,—and has left a fortune to my
daughter. Well, I refuse it. There is no occasion for further parley. I refuse it. Dora, show
this gentleman downstairs."

"There is only one thing to be said," said the
visitor, rising, "you have not the power to refuse
it. It is vested in trustees, of whom I am one.

The young lady herself may take any foolish step —if you will allow me to say so—when she comes of age. But you have not the power to do this. The allowance to be made to her during her minority and all other particulars will be settled as soon as the arrangements are sufficiently advanced."

"I tell you that I refuse it," repeated Mr. Mannering.

"And I repeat that you have no power to do so. I leave her the directions in respect to the other event, in which you have full power. I implore you to use it mercifully," the visitor said.

He went away without any further farewell— Mannering, not moving, sitting at the table with his eyes fixed on the empty air. Dora, who had followed the conversation with astonished un- comprehension, but with an acute sense of the incivility with which the stranger had been treated, hurried to open the door for him, to offer him her hand, to make what apologies were possible.

" Father has been very ill," she said. " He nearly died. This is the first time he has been out of his room. I don't understand what it all means, but please do not think he is uncivil. He is excited, and still ill and weak. I never in my life saw him rude to any one before."

"Never mind," said the old gentleman, pausing outside the door ; " I can make allowances. You and I may have a great deal to do with each other, Miss Dora. I hope you will have confidence in me ? "

" I don't know what it all means," Dora said.

"No, but some day you will; and in the meantime remember that some one, who has the best right to do so, has left you a great deal of money, and that whenever you want anything, or even wish for anything, you must come to me."

"A great deal of money?" Dora said. She had

heard him speak of a fortune—a considerable fortune, but the words had not struck her as these did.   A great deal of money?   And money was all that was wanted to make everything smooth, and open out vistas of peace and pleasure, where all had been trouble and care.   The sudden lighting up of her countenance was as if the sun had come out all at once from among the clouds.   The old gentleman, who, like so many old gentlemen, entertained cynical views, chuckled to see that even at this youthful age, and in Mannering's daughter, who had refused it so fiercely, the name of a great deal of money should light up a girl's face.   " They are all alike," he said to himself as he went downstairs.

When Dora returned to the room, she found her father as she had left him, staring straight before him, seeing nothing, his head supported on his hands, his hollow eyes fixed.   He did not notice her return, as he had not noticed her absence.

What was she to do? One of those crises had arrived which are so petty, yet so important, when the wisest of women are reduced to semi-imbecility by an emergency not contemplated in any moral code. It was time for him to take his beef tea. The doctor had commanded that under no circumstances was this duty to be omitted or postponed ; but who could have foreseen such circumstances as these, in which evidently matters of life and death were going through his mind? After such an agitating interview he wanted it more and more, the nourishment upon which his recovery depended. But how suggest it to a man whose mind was gone away into troubled roamings through the past, or still more troubled questions about the future? It could have been no small matters that had been brought back to Mr. Mannering's mind by that strange visit. Dora, who was not weak-minded, trembled to approach him with any prosaic, petty suggestion. And yet

how did she dare to pass it by? Dora went
about the room very quietly, longing to rouse yet
unwilling to disturb him.   How was she to speak
of such a small matter as his beef tea?   And yet
it was not a small matter.   She heard Gilchrist
go into the other room, bringing it all ready on
the little tray, and hurried thither to inquire what
that experienced woman would advise.   " He has
had some one to see him about business.   He has
been very much put out, dreadfully disturbed.   I
don't know how to tell you how much.   His
mind is full of some dreadful thing I don't understand.   How can I ask him to take his beef
tea?   And yet he must want it.   He is looking
so ill.   He is so worn out.   Oh, Gilchrist, what
am I to do?"

    " It is just a very hard question, Miss Dora.
He should not have seen any person on business.
He's no' in a fit state to see anybody the first day
he is out of his bedroom : though, for my part, I

think he might have been out of his bedroom three or four days ago," Gilchrist said.

"As if that was the question now! The question is about the beef tea. Can I go and say, 'Father, never mind whatever has happened, there is nothing so important as your beef tea'? Can I tell him that everything else may come and go, but that beef tea runs on for ever? Oh, Gilchrist, you are no good at all! Tell me what to do."

Dora could not help being light-hearted, though it was in the present circumstances so inappropriate, when she thought of that "great deal of money"—money that would sweep all bills away, that would make almost everything possible. That consciousness lightened more and more upon her, as she saw the little bundle of bills carefully labelled and tied up, which she had intended to remove surreptitiously from her father's room while he was out of it. With what comfort and satisfaction could she remove them now!

"Just put it down on the table by his side, Miss Dora," said Gilchrist. "Say no word, just put it there within reach of his hand. Maybe he will fly out at you, and ask if you think there's nothing in the world so important as your con-founded—— But no, he will not say that; he's no' a man that gets relief in that way. But, on the other hand, he will maybe just be conscious that there's a good smell, and he will feel he's wanting something, and he will drink it off without more ado. But do not, Miss Dora, whatever you do, let more folk on business bother your poor papaw, for I could not answer for what might come of it. You had better let me sit here on the watch, and see that nobody comes near the door."

"I will do what you say, and you can do what you like," said Dora. She could almost have danced along the passage. Poor lady from

America, who was dead! Dora had been very sorry. She had been much troubled by the interview about her which she did not understand: but even if father were pitiless, which was so incredible, it could do that poor woman no harm now: and the money—money which would be deliverance, which would pay all the bills, and leave the quarter's money free to go to the country with, to go abroad with! Dora had to tone her countenance down, not to look too guiltily glad when she went in to where her father was sitting in the same abstraction and gloom. But this time he observed her entrance, looking up as if he had been waiting for her. She had barely time to follow Gilchrist's directions when he stretched out his hand and took hers, drawing her near to him. He was very grave and pale, but no longer so terrible as before.

"Dora," he said, "how often have you seen this lady of whom I have heard to-day?"

"Twice, father; once in Miss Bethune's room, where she had come, I don't know how."

"In this house?" he said with a strong quiver, which Dora felt, as if it had been communicated to herself.

"And the night before last, when Miss Bethune took me to where she was living, a long way off, by Hyde Park. I knelt at the bed a long time, and then they put me in a chair. She said many things I did not understand—but chiefly," Dora said, her eyes filling with tears—the scene seemed to come before her more touchingly in recollection than when, to her wonder and dismay, it took place, "chiefly that she loved me, that she had wanted me all my life, and that she wished for me above everything before she died."

"And then?" he said, with a catch in his breath.

"I don't know, father; I was so confused and

dizzy with being there so long. All of a sudden they took me away, and the others all came round the bed. And then there was nothing more. Miss Bethune brought me home. I understood that the lady—that my poor—my poor aunt—if that is what she was—was dead. Oh, father, whatever she did, forgive her now!"

Dora for the moment had forgotten everything but the pity and the wonder, which she only now began to realise for the first time, of that strange scene. She saw, as if for the first time, the dark room, the twinkling lights, the ineffable smile upon the dying face : and her big tears fell fast upon her father's hand, which held hers in a trembling grasp. The quiver that was in him ran through and through her, so that she trembled too.

"Dora," he said, "perhaps you ought to know, as that man said. The lady was not your aunt : she was your mother — my" — there seemed a convulsion in his throat, as though he could not pronounce the word—"my wife. And yet she was not to blame, as the world judges. I went on a long expedition after you were born, leaving her very young still, and poor. I did not mean her to be poor. I did not mean to be long away. But I went to Africa, which is terrible enough now, but was far more terrible in those days. I fell ill again and again. I was left behind for dead. I was lost in those dreadful wilds. It was more than three years before I came to the light of day at all, and it seemed a hundred. I had been given up by everybody. The money had failed her, her people were poor, the Museum gave her a small allowance as to the widow of a man killed in its service. And there was another man who loved her. They meant no harm, it is true. She did nothing that was wrong. She married him, thinking I was dead."

"Father!" Dora cried, clasping his arm with both her hands : his other arm supported his head.

"It was a pity that I was not dead—that was the pity. If I had known, I should never have come back to put everything wrong. But I never heard a word till I came back. And she would not face me—never. She fled as if she had been guilty. She was not guilty, you know. She had only married again, which the best of women do. She fled by herself at first, leaving you to me. She said it was all she could do, but that she never, never could look me in the face again. It has not been that I could not forgive her, Dora. No, but we could not look each other in the face again."

"Is it she," said Dora, struggling to speak, "whose picture is in your cabinet, on its face? May I take it, father? I should like to have it."

He put his other arm round her and pressed her close. "And after this," he said, "my little girl, we will never say a word on this subject again."

CHAPTER XIX.

THE little old gentleman had withdrawn from the apartment of the Mannerings very quietly, leaving all that excitement and commotion behind him; but he did not leave in this way the house in Bloomsbury. He went downstairs cautiously and quietly, though why he should have done so he could not himself have told, since, had he made all the noise in the world, it could have had no effect upon the matter in hand in either case. Then he knocked at Miss Bethune's door. When he was bidden to enter, he opened the door gently, with great precaution, and going in, closed it with equal care behind him.

"I am speaking, I think, to Mrs. Gordon Grant?" he said.

Miss Bethune was alone. She had many

things to think of, and very likely the book which she seemed to be reading was not much more than a pretence to conceal her thoughts. It fell down upon her lap at these words, and she looked at her questioner with a gasp, unable to make any reply.

"Mrs. Gordon Grant, I believe?" he said again, then made a step farther into the room. "Pardon me for startling you, there is no one here. I am a solicitor, John Templar, of Gray's Inn. Precautions taken with other persons need not apply to me. You are Mrs. Gordon Grant, I know."

"I have never borne that name," she said, very pale. "Janet Bethune, that is my name."

"Not as signed to a document which is in my possession. You will pardon me, but this is no doing of mine. You witnessed Mrs. Bristow's will?"

She gave a slight nod with her head in acquiescence.

" And then, to my great surprise, I found this name, which I have been in search of for so long."

" You have been in search of it ? "

" Yes, for many years. The skill with which you have concealed it is wonderful. I have advertised, even. I have sought the help of old friends who must see you often, who come to you here even, I know. But I never found the name I was in search of, never till the other day at the signing of Mrs. Bristow's will—which, by the way," he said, "that young fellow might have signed safely enough, for he has no share in it."

" Do you mean to say that she has left him nothing—nothing, Mr. Templar? The boy that was like her son ! "

" Not a penny," said the old gentleman—" not a penny. Everything has gone the one way— perhaps it was not wonderful—to her own child."

" I could not have done that ! " cried the lady.

"Oh, I could not have done it! I would have felt it would bring a curse upon my own child."

"Perhaps, madam, you never had a child of your own, which would make all the difference," he said.

She looked at him again, silent, with her lips pressed very closely together, and a kind of defiance in her eyes.

"But this," he said again, softly, "is no answer to my question. You were a witness of Mrs. Bristow's will, and you signed a certain name to it. You cannot have done so hoping to vitiate the document by a feigned name. It would have been perfectly futile to begin with, and no woman could have thought of such a thing. That was, I presume, your lawful name?"

"It is a name I have never borne; that you will very easily ascertain."

"Still it is your name, or why should you have signed it—in inadvertence, I suppose?"

"Not certainly in inadvertence. Has anything ever made it familiar to me? If you will
know, I had my reasons. I thought the sight of
it might put things in a lawyer's hands, would
maybe guide inquiries, would make easier an
object of my own."

"That object," said Mr. Templar, "was to
discover your husband?"

She half rose to her feet, flushed and angry.

"Who said I had a husband, or that to find
him or lose him was anything to me?" Then,
with a strong effort, she reseated herself in her
chair. "That was a bold guess," she said, "Mr.
Templar, not to say a little insulting, don't you
think, to a respectable single lady that has never
had a finger lifted upon her? I am of a well-
known race enough. I have never concealed
myself. There are plenty of people in Scotland
who will give you full details of me and all my
ways. It is not like a lawyer—a cautious man,

bound by his profession to be careful--to make such a strange attempt upon me."

"I make no attempt. I only ask a question, and one surely most justifiable. You did not sign a name to which you had no right, on so important a document as a will; therefore you are Mrs. Gordon Grant, and a person to whom for many years I have had a statement to make."

She looked at him again with a dumb rigidity of aspect, but said not a word.

"The communication I had to make to you," he said, "was of a death—not one, so far as I know, that could bring you any advantage, or harm either, I suppose. I may say that it took place years ago. I have no reason, either, to suppose that it would be the cause of any deep sorrow."

"Sorrow?" she said, but her lips were dry, and could articulate no more.

"I have nothing to do with your reasons for

having kept your marriage so profound a secret,"
he said. "The result has naturally been the long
delay of a piece of information which perhaps
would have been welcome to you. Mrs. Grant,
your husband, George Gordon Grant, died nearly
twenty years ago."

"Twenty years ago!" she cried, with a start,
"twenty years?" Then she raised her voice
suddenly and cried, "Gilchrist!" She was very
pale, and her excitement great, her eyes gleaming,
her nerves quivering. She paid no attention to
the little lawyer, who on his side observed her so
closely. "Gilchrist," she said, when the maid
came in hurriedly from the inner room in which
she had been, "we have often wondered why there
was no sign of him when I came into my fortune.
The reason is he was dead before my uncle died."

"Dead?" said Gilchrist, and put up at once
her apron to her eyes, "dead? Oh, mem, that
bonnie young man!"

"Yes," said Miss Bethune. She rose up and began to move about the room in great excitement. "Yes, he would still be a bonnie young man then—oh, a bonnie young man, as his son is now. I wondered how it was he made no sign. Before, it was natural : but when my uncle was dead—when I had come into my fortune! That explains it—that explains it all. He was dead before the day he had reckoned on came."

"Oh, dinna say that, now!" cried Gilchrist. "How can we tell if it was the day he had reckoned on? Why might it no' be your comfort he was aye thinking of—that you might lose nothing, that your uncle might keep his faith in you, that your fortune might be safe?"

"Ay, that my fortune might be safe, that was the one thing. What did it matter about me? Only a woman that was so silly as to believe in him—and believed in him, God help me, long after he had proved what he was. Gilchrist, go

down on your knees and thank God that he did
not live to cheat us more, to come when you and
me made sure he would come, and fleece us with
his fair face and his fair ways, till he had got
what he wanted,—the filthy money which was the
end of all."

"Oh, mem," cried Gilchrist, again weeping,
"dinna say that now. Even if it were true,
which the Lord forbid, dinna say it now!"

But her mistress was not to be controlled.
The stream of recollection, of pent-up feeling, the
brooding of a lifetime, set free by this sudden
discovery of her story, which was like the breaking down of a dyke to a river, rushed forth like
that river in flood. "I have thought many a
time," she cried,—"when my heart was sick of
the silence, when I still trembled that he would
come, and wished he would come for all that I
knew, like a fool woman that I am, as all women
are,—that maybe his not coming was a sign of

grace, that he had maybe forgotten, maybe been untrue ; but that it was not at least the money, the money and nothing more. To know that I had that accursed siller and not to come for it was a sign of grace. I was a kind of glad. But it was not that!" she cried, pacing to and fro like a wild creature,—"it was not that! He would have come, oh, and explained everything, made everything clear, and told me to my face it was for my sake!—if it had not been that death stepped in and disappointed him as he had disappointed me!"

Miss Bethune ended with a harsh laugh, and after a moment seated herself again in her chair. The tempest of personal feeling had carried her away, quenching even the other and yet stronger sentiment, which for so many years had been the passion of her life. She had been suddenly, strangely driven back to a period which even now, in her sober middle age, it was a kind of madness to think of--the years which she had lived through in awful silence, a wife yet no wife, a mother yet no mother, cut off from everything but the monotonous, prolonged, unending formula of a girlhood out of date, the life without individuality, without meaning, and without hope, of a large-minded and active woman, kept to the rôle of a child, in a house where there was not even affection to sweeten it. The recollection of those terrible, endless, changeless days, running into years as indistinguishable, the falsehood of every circumstance and appearance, the secret existence of love and sacrifice, of dread knowledge and disenchantment, of strained hope and failing illusion, and final and awful despair, of which Gilchrist alone knew anything,—Gilchrist, the faithful servant, the sole companion of her heart,—came back upon her with all that horrible sense of the intolerable which such a martyrdom brings. She had borne it in its day—how had she borne it?

Was it possible that a woman could go through that and live? her heart torn from her bosom, her baby torn from her side, and no one, no one but Gilchrist, to keep a little life alive in her heart! And it had lasted for years—many, many, many years,—all the years of her life, except those first twenty which tell for so little. In that rush of passion she did not know how time passed, whether it was five minutes or an hour that she sat under the inspection of the old lawyer, whom this puzzle of humanity filled with a sort of professional interest, and who did not think it necessary to withdraw, or had any feeling of intrusion upon the sufferer. It was not really a long time, though it might have been a year, when she roused herself and took hold of her forces, and the dread panorama rolled away.

Gradually the familiar things around her came back. She remembered herself, no despairing girl, no soul in bondage, but a sober woman, disen-

chanted in many ways, but never yet cured of
those hopes and that faith which hold the ardent
spirit to life. Her countenance changed with her
thoughts, her eyes ceased to be abstracted and
visionary, her colour came back. She turned to
the old gentleman with a look which for the first
time disturbed and bewildered that old and hard-
ened spectator of the vicissitudes of life. Her eyes
filled with a curious liquid light, an expression
wistful, flattering, entreating. She looked at him
as a child looks who has a favour to ask, her head
a little on one side, her lips quivering with a smile.
There came into the old lawyer's mind, he could
not tell how, a ridiculous sense of being a superior
being, a kind of god, able to confer untold advantages and favours. What did the woman want of
him? What—it did not matter what she wanted—
could he do for her? Nothing that he was aware
of: and a sense of the danger of being cajoled came
into his mind, but along with that, which was

ridiculous, though he could not help it, a sense of being really a superior being, able to grant favours, and benignant, as he had never quite known himself to be.

"Mr. Templar," she said, "now all is over there is not another word to say : and now the boy—my boy ——"

" The boy ? " he repeated, with a surprised air.

" My child that was taken from me as soon as he was born, my little helpless bairn that never knew his mother—my son, my son ! Give me a right to him, give me my lawful title to him, and there can be no more doubt about it—that nobody may say he is not mine."

The old lawyer was more confused than words could say. The very sense she had managed to convey to his mind of being a superior being, full of graces and gifts to confer, made his downfall the more ludicrous to himself. He seemed to tumble down from an altitude quite visionary, yet very real, as if by some neglect or ill-will of his own.   He felt himself humiliated, a culprit before her.   " My dear lady," he said, "you are going too fast and too far for me.   I did not even know there was any —— Stop! I think I begin to remember."

" Yes," she said, breathless,—" yes!" looking at him with supplicating eyes.

" Now it comes back to me," he said.   " I—I —am afraid I gave it no importance.   There was a baby—yes, a little thing a few weeks, or a few months old—that died."

She sprang up again once more to her feet, menacing, terrible.   She was bigger, stronger, far more full of life, than he was.   She towered over him, her face full of tragic passion.   " It is not true—it is not true!" she cried.

" My dear lady, how can I know?   What can I do? I can but tell you the instructions given to me; it had slipped out of my mind, it seemed

of little importance in comparison.   A baby that
was too delicate to bear the separation from its
mother—I remember it all now.   I am very sorry,
very sorry, if I have conveyed any false hopes to
your mind.   The baby died not long after it was
taken away."

"It is not true," Miss Bethune said, with a
hoarse and harsh voice.   After the excitement
and passion, she stood like a figure cut out of
stone.   This statement, so calm and steady,
struck her like a blow.   Her lips denied, but her
heart received the cruel news.   It may be necessary to explain good fortune, but misery comes
with its own guarantee.   It struck her like a
sword, like a scythe, shearing down her hopes.
She rose into a brief blaze of fury, denying it.
"Oh, you think I will believe that?" she cried,
—"me that have followed him in my thoughts
through every stage, have seen him grow and
blossom and come to be a man!   Do you think

there would have been no angel to stop me in my
vain imaginations, no kind creature in heaven or
earth that would have breathed into my heart and
said, 'Go on no more, hope no more'? Oh no—
oh no! Heaven is not like that, nor earth! Pain
comes and trouble, but not cruel fate. No, I do not
believe it—I will not believe it! It is not true."

"My dear lady," said the old gentleman, dis-
tressed.

"I am no dear lady to you. I am nothing to
you. I am a poor, deserted, heartbroken woman,
that have lived false, false, but never meant it:
that have had no one to stand by me, to help me
out of it. And now you sit there calm, and look
me in the face, and take away my son. My baby
first was taken from me, forced out of my arms,
new-born: and now you take the boy I've followed with my heart these long, long years, the
bonnie lad, the young man I've seen. I tell you
I've seen him, then. How can a mother be de-

ceived? We've seen him, both Gilchrist and me. Ask her, if you doubt my word. We have seen him, can any lie stand against that? And my heart has spoken, and his heart has spoken; we have sought each other in the dark, and taken hands. I know him by his bonnie eyes, and a trick in his mouth that is just my father over again : and he knows me by nature, and the touch of kindly blood."

"Oh, mem," Gilchrist cried, " I warned ye—I warned ye! What is a likeness to lippen to? And I never saw it," the woman said, with tears.

" And who asked ye to see it, or thought ye could see it, a serving-woman, not a drop's blood to him or to me? It would be a bonnie thing," said Miss Bethune, pausing, looking round, as if to appeal to an unseen audience, with an almost smile of scorn, "if my hired woman's word was to be taken instead of his mother's. Did she bear him in pain and anguish? Did she wait for him, lying dreaming, month after month, that he was to cure all? She got him in her arms when he was born, but he had been in mine for long before; he had grown a man in my heart before ever he saw the light of day. Oh, ask her, and there is many a fable she will tell ye. But me!"—she calmed down again, a smile came upon her face,— "I have seen my son. Now, as I have nobody but him, he has nobody but me : and I mean from this day to take him home and acknowledge him before all the world."

Mr. Templar had risen, and stood with his hand on the back of his chair. "I have nothing more to say," he said. "If I can be of any use to you in any way, command me, madam. It is no wish of mine to take any comfort from you, or even to dispel any pleasing illusion."

"As if you could!" she said, rising again, proud and smiling. "As if any old lawyer's words, as dry as dust, could shake my conviction, or persuade me out of what is a certainty.   It is a certainty.   Seeing is believing, the very vulgar say.   And I have seen him—do you think you could make me believe after that, that there is no one to see?"

He shook his head and turned away.   "Good-morning to you, ma'am," he said.   "I have told you the truth, but I cannot make you believe it, and why should I try?   It may be happier for you the other way."

"Happier?" she said, with a laugh.   "Ay, because it's true.   Falsehood has been my fate too long—I am happy because it is true."

Miss Bethune sat down again, when her visitor closed the door behind him.   The triumph and brightness gradually died out of her face. "What are you greetin' there for, you fool?" she said, "and me the happiest woman, and the proudest mother!   Gilchrist," she said, suddenly turning round upon her maid, "the woman that is

dead was a weak creature, bound hand and foot
all her life. She meant no harm, poor thing, I
will allow, but yet she broke one man's life in
pieces, and it must have been a poor kind of
happiness she gave the other, with her heart
always straying after another man's bairn. And
I've done nothing, nothing to injure any mortal.
I was true till I could be true no longer, till he
showed all he was ; and true I have been in spite
of that all my life, and endured and never said a
word. Do you think it's possible, possible that
yon woman should be rewarded with her child in
her arms, and her soul satisfied?—and me left
desolate, with my very imaginations torn from me,
torn out of me, and my heart left bleeding, and all
my thoughts turned into lies, like myself, that
have been no better than a lie?—turned into lies?"

"Oh, mem!" cried Gilchrist—"oh, my dear
leddy, that has been more to me than a' this
world! Is it for me to say that it's no' justice we

have to expect, for we deserve nothing ; and that the Lord knows His ain reasons ; and that the time will come when we'll get it all back—you, your bairn, the Lord bless him ! and me to see ye as happy as the angels, which is all I ever wanted or thought to get either here or otherwhere!"

CHAPTER XX.

THERE was nothing more said to Mr. Mannering on the subject of Mr. Templar's mission, neither did he himself say anything, either to sanction or prevent his child from carrying out the strange desire of her mother—her mother! Dora did not accept the thought. She made a struggle within herself to keep up the fiction that it was her mother's sister—a relation, something near, yet ever inferior to the vision of a benignant, melancholy being, unknown, which a dead mother so often is to an imaginative girl.

It pleased her to find, as she said to herself, "no likeness" to the suffering and hysterical woman she had seen, in that calm, pensive portrait, which she instantly secured and took possession of—the little picture which had lain so long buried with its face downward in the secret drawer. She gazed at it for an hour together, and found nothing—nothing, she declared to herself with indignant satisfaction, to remind her of the other face—flushed, weeping, middle-aged —which had so implored her affection. Had it been her mother, was it possible that it should have required an effort to give that affection? No! Dora at sixteen believed very fully in the voice of nature. It would have been impossible, her heart at once would have spoken, she would have known by some infallible instinct. She put the picture up in her own room, and filled her heart with the luxury, the melancholy, the sadness, and pleasure of this possession—her mother's portrait, more touching to the imagination than any other image could be. But then there began to steal a little shadow over Dora's thoughts. She would not give up her determined resistance to the idea that this face and the other face, living and dying, which she had seen, could be one; but when she raised her eyes suddenly, to her mother's picture, a consciousness would steal over her, an involuntary glance of recognition. What more likely than that there should be a resemblance, faint and far away, between sister and sister? And then there came to be a gleam of reproach to Dora in those eyes, and the girl began to feel as if there was an irreverence, a want of feeling, in turning that long recluse and covered face to the light of day, and carrying on all the affairs of life under it, as if it were a common thing. Finally she arranged over it a little piece of drapery, a morsel of faded embroidered silk which was among her treasures, soft and faint in its colours—a veil which she could draw in her moments of thinking and quiet, those moments which it would not be irreverent any longer to call a dead mother or an angelic presence to hallow and to share.

But she said nothing when she was called to Miss Bethune's room, and clad in mourning, recognising with a thrill, half of horror, half of pride, the crape upon her dress which proved her right to that new exaltation among human creatures—that position of a mourner which is in its way a step in life. Dora did not ask where she was going when she followed Miss Bethune, also in black from head to foot, to the plain little brougham which had been ordered to do fit and solemn honour to the occasion ; the great white wreath and basket of flowers, which filled up the space, called no observation from her. They drove in silence to the great cemetery, with all its gay flowers and elaborate aspect of cheerfulness. It was a fine but cloudy day, warm and soft, yet without sunshine ; and Dora had a curious sense of importance, of meaning, as if she had attained an advanced stage of being. Already an experience had fallen to her share, more than one experience. She had knelt, troubled and awe-stricken, by a death-bed ; she was now going to stand by a grave. Even where real sorrow exists, this curious sorrowful elation of sentiment is apt to come into the mind of the very young. Dora was deeply impressed by the circumstances and the position, but it was impossible that she could feel any real grief. Tears came to her eyes as she dropped the shower of flowers, white and lovely, into the darkness of that last abode. Her face was full of awe and pity, but her breast of that vague, inexplainable expansion and growth, as of a creature entered into the larger developments and knowledge of life. There were very few other mourners. Mr. Templar, the lawyer, with his keen but veiled observation of everything, serious and businesslike ; the doctor, with professional gravity and indifference ; Miss Bethune, with almost stern seriousness, standing like a statue in her black dress and with her pale

face.   Why should any of these spectators care?
The woman was far the most moved, thinking of
the likeness and difference of her own fate, of the
failure of that life which was now over, and of her
own, a deeper failure still, without any fault of
hers.   And Dora, wondering, developing, her
eyes full of abstract tears, and her mind of awe.

Only one mourner stood pale with watching and
thought beside the open grave, his heart aching
with loneliness and a profound natural vacancy
and pain.   He knew that she had neglected him,
almost wronged him at the last, cut him off, taking
no thought of what was to become of him.   He
felt even that in so doing this woman was unfaith-
ful to her trust, and had done what she ought not
to have done.   But all that mattered nothing in
face of natural sorrow, natural love.   She had
been a mother to him, and she was gone.   The
ear always open to his boyish talk and confidence,
always ready to listen, could hear him no more;

and, almost more poignant, his care of her was
over, there was nothing more to do for her, none
of the hundred commissions that used to send him
flying, the hundred things that had to be done.
His occupation in life seemed to be over, his home,
his natural place. It had not perhaps ever been
a natural place, but he had not felt that. She had
been his mother, though no drop of her blood ran
in his veins; and now he was nobody's son, belonging to no family. The other people round looked
like ghosts to Harry Gordon. They were part of
the strange cutting off, the severance he already
felt; none of them had anything to do with her,
and yet it was he who was pushed out and put
aside, as if he had nothing to do with her, the only
mother he had ever known! The little sharp old
lawyer was her representative now, not he who
had been her son. He stood languid, in a moment of utter depression, collapse of soul and
body, by the grave. When all was over, and the

solemn voice which sounds as no other voice ever
does, falling calm through the still air, bidding
earth return to earth, and dust to dust, had ceased,
he still stood as if unable to comprehend that all
was over—no one to bid him come away, no other
place to go to. His brain was not relieved by
tears, or his mind set in activity by anything to
do. He stood there half stupefied, left behind, in
that condition when simply to remain as we are
seems the only thing possible to us.

Miss Bethune had placed Dora in the little
brougham, in rigorous fulfilment of her duty to
the child. Mr. Templar and the doctor had both
departed, the two other women, Mrs. Bristow's
maid and the nurse who had accompanied her,
had driven away : and still the young man stood,
not paying any attention. Miss Bethune waited
for a little by the carriage door. She did not
answer the appeal of the coachman, asking if he
was to drive away ; she said nothing to Dora,

whose eyes endeavoured in vain to read the
changes in her friend's face ; but, after standing
there for a few minutes quite silent, she suddenly
turned and went back to the cemetery. It was
strange to her to hesitate in anything she did,
and from the moment she left the carriage door
all uncertainty was over. She went back with a
quick step, treading her way among the graves,
and put her hand upon young Gordon's arm.

"You are coming home with me," she said.

The new, keen voice, irregular and full of life,
so unlike the measured tones to which he had
been listening, struck the young man uneasily in
the midst of his melancholy reverie, which was
half trance, half exhaustion. He moved a step
away, as if to shake off the interruption, scarcely
conscious what, and not at all who it was.

"My dear young man, you must come home
with me," she said again.

He looked at her, with consciousness re-awakening, and attempted to smile, with his natural ready response to every kindness. " It is you," he said, and then, " I might have known it could only be you."

What did that mean? Nothing at all. Merely his sense that the one person who had spoken kindly to him, looked tenderly at him (though he had never known why, and had been both amused and embarrassed by the consciousness), was the most likely among all the strangers by whom he was surrounded to be kind to him now. But it produced an effect upon Miss Bethune which was far beyond any meaning it bore.

A great light seemed suddenly to blaze over her face ; her eyes, which had been so veiled and stern, awoke; every line of a face which could be harsh and almost rigid in repose, began to melt and soften ; her composure, which had been almost solemn, failed ; her lip began to quiver, tears came dropping upon his arm, which she

suddenly clasped with both her hands, clinging to
it. "You say right," she cried, "my dear, my
dear!—more right than all the reasons. It is you
and nature that makes everything clear. You are
just coming home with me."

"I don't seem," he said, "to know what the
word means."

"But you will soon learn again. God bless
the good woman that cherished you and loved
you, my bonnie boy. I'll not say a word against
her—oh, no, no! God's blessing upon her as she
lies there. I will never grudge a good word you
say of her, never a regret. But now"—she put
her arm within his with a proud and tender
movement, which so far penetrated his languor
as to revive the bewilderment which he had felt
before—"now you are coming home with me."

He did not resist; he allowed himself to be
led to the little carriage and packed into it, which
was not quite an easy thing to do. On another

occasion he would have laughed and protested;
but on this he submitted gravely to whatever was
required of him, thankful, in the failure of all
motive, to have some one to tell him what to do,
to move him as if he were an automaton.   He sat
bundled up on the little front seat, with Dora's
wondering countenance opposite to him, and that
other inexplicable face, inspired and lighted up
with tenderness.   He had not strength enough to
inquire why this stranger took possession of him
so; neither could Dora tell, who sat opposite to
him, her mind awakened, her thoughts busy.
This was the almost son of the woman who they
said was Dora's mother.   What was he to Dora?
Was he the nearer to her, or the farther from her,
for that relationship?   Did she like him better or
worse for having done everything that it ought,
they said, have been her part to do?

These questions were all confused in Dora's
mind, but they were not favourable to this new

interloper into her life—he who had known about her for years while she had never heard of him. She sat very upright, reluctant to make room for him, yet scrupulously doing so, and a little indignant that he should thus be brought in to interfere with her own claims to the first place. The drive to Bloomsbury seemed very long in these circumstances, and it was indeed a long drive. They all came back into the streets after the long suburban road with a sense almost of relief in the growing noise, the rattle of the causeway, and sound of the carts and carriages — which made it unnecessary, as it had been impossible for them, to say anything to each other, and brought back the affairs of common life to dispel the influences of the solemn moment that was past.

When they had reached Miss Bethune's rooms, and returned altogether to existence, and the sight of a table spread for a meal, it was a shock, but

not an ungrateful one. Miss Bethune at once
threw off the gravity which had wrapped her like
a cloak, when she put away her black bonnet.
She bade Gilchrist hurry to have the luncheon
brought up. "These two young creatures have
eaten nothing, I am sure, this day. Probably
they think they cannot: but when food is set
before them they will learn better. Haste ye,
Gilchrist, to have it served up. No, Dora, you
will stay with me too. Your father is a troubled
man this day. You will not go in upon him with
that cloud about you, not till you are refreshed
and rested, and have got your colour and your
natural look back. And you, my bonnie man!"
She could not refrain from touching, caressing his
shoulder as she passed him; her eyes kept filling
with tears as she looked at him. He for his part
moved and took his place as she told him, still in
a dream.

It was a curious meal, more daintily prepared

and delicate than usual, and Miss Bethune was a woman who at all times was "very particular," and exercised all the gifts of the landlady, whose other lodgers demanded much less of her. And the mistress of the little feast was still less as usual. She scarcely sat down at her own table, but served her young guests with anxious care, carving choice morsels for them, watching their faces, their little movements of impatience, and the gradual development of natural appetite, which came as the previous spell gradually wore off. She talked all the time, her countenance a little flushed and full of emotion, her eyes moist and shining, with frequent sallies at Gilchrist, who hovered round the table waiting upon the young guests, and in her excitement making continual mistakes and stumblings, which soon roused Dora to laugh, and Harry to apologise.

"It is all right," he cried, when Miss Bethune at last made a dart at her attendant, and gave her, what is called in feminine language, "a shake," to bring her to herself.

"Are you out of your wits, woman?" Miss Bethune exclaimed. "Go away and leave me to look after the bairns, if ye cannot keep your head. Are you out of your wits?"

"Indeed, mem, and I have plenty of reason," Gilchrist said, weeping, and feeling for her apron, while the dish in her hand wavered wildly; and then it was that Harry Gordon, coming to himself, cried out that it was all right.

"And I am going to have some of that," he added, steadying the kind creature, whose instinct of service had more effect than either encouragement or reproof. And this little touch of reality settled him too. He began to respond a little, to rouse himself, even to see the humour of the situation, at which Dora had begun to laugh, but which brought a soft moisture, in which was ease and consolation, to his eyes.

It was not until about an hour later that Miss Bethune was left alone with the young man. He had begun by this time to speak about himself. " I am not so discouraged as you think," he said, " I don't seem to be afraid. After all, it doesn't matter much, does it, what happens to a young fellow all alone in the world? It's only me, anyhow. I have no wife," he said, with a faint laugh, "no sister to be involved—nothing but my own rather useless person, a thing of no account. It wasn't that that knocked me down. It was just the feeling of the end of everything, and that she was laid there that had been so good to me—so good—and nothing ever to be done for her any more."

" I can forgive you that," said Miss Bethune, with a sort of sob in her throat. " And yet she was ill to you, unjust at the last."

" No, not that. I have had everything, too much for a man capable of earning his living to accept—but then it seemed all so natural, it was the common course of life. I was scarcely waking up to see that it could not be."

"And a cruel rousing you have had at last, my poor boy."

"No," he said steadily, "I will never allow it was cruel; it has been sharp and effectual. It couldn't help being effectual, could it? since I have no alternative. The pity is I am good for so little. No education to speak of."

"You shall have education—as much as you can set your face to."

He looked up at her with a little air of surprise, and shook his head. "No," he said, "not now. I am too old. I must lose no more time. The thing is, that my work will be worth so much less, being guided by no skill. Skill is a beautiful thing. I envy the very scavengers," he said (who were working underneath the window), "for piling up their mud like that, straight. I should

never get it straight." The poor young fellow
was so near tears that he was glad from time to
time to have a chance of a feeble laugh, which
relieved him. "And that is humble enough! I
think much the best thing for me will be to go
back to South America. There are people who
know me, who would give me a little place where
I could learn. Book-keeping can't be such a
tremendous mystery. There's an old clerk or
two of my guardians "—here he paused to swallow down the climbing sorrow—"who would
give me a hint or two. And if the pay was very
small at first, why, I'm not an . extravagant
fellow."

"Are you sure of that?" his confidante said.

He looked at her again, surprised, then
glanced at himself and his dress, which was not
economical, and reddened and laughed again. "I
am afraid you are right," he said. "I haven't
known much what economy was. I have lived

like the other people; but I am not too old to
learn, and I should not mind in the least what I
looked like, or how I lived, for a time. Things
would get better after a time."

They were standing together near the window,
for he had begun to roam about the room as he
talked, and she had risen from her chair with one
of the sudden movements of excitement. "There
will be no need," she said,—"there will be no
need. Something will be found for you at home."

He shook his head. "You forget it is scarcely
home to me. And what could I do here that
would be worth paying me for? I must no more
be dependent upon kindness. Oh, don't think
I do not feel kindness. What should I have
done this miserable day but for you, who have
been so good to me—as good as—as a mother,
though I had no claim?"

She gave a great cry, and seized him by both
his hands. "Oh, lad, if you knew what you were

saying! That word to me, that have died for it, and have no claim! Gilchrist, Gilchrist!" she cried, suddenly dropping his hands again, "come here and speak to me! Help me! have pity upon me! For if this is not him, all nature and God's against me. Come here before I speak or die!"

CHAPTER XXI.

IT was young Gordon himself, alarmed but not excited as by any idea of a new discovery which could affect his fate, who brought Miss Bethune back to herself, far better than Gilchrist could do, who had no art but to weep and entreat, and then yield to her mistress whatever she might wish. *A quelque chose malheur est bon.* He had been in the habit of soothing and calming down an excitable, sometimes hysterical woman, whose *accés des nerfs* meant nothing, or were, at least, supposed to mean nothing, except indeed nerves, and the ups and downs which are characteristic of them. He was roused by the not dissimilar outburst of feeling or passion, wholly incomprehensible to him from any other point of view, to which his new friend had given way. He took it

very quietly, with the composure of use and wont.
The sight of her emotion and excitement brought
him quite back to himself. He could imagine no
reason whatever for it, except the sympathetic
effect of all the troublous circumstances in which
she had been, without any real reason, involved.
It was her sympathy, her kindness for himself
and for Dora, he had not the least doubt, which,
by bringing her into those scenes of pain and
trouble, and associating her so completely with
the complicated and intricate story, had brought
on this "attack". What he had known to be
characteristic of the one woman with whom he
had been in familiar intercourse for so long a
period of his life seemed to Harry characteristic
of all women. He was quite equal to the occasion. Dr. Roland himself, who would have been
so full of professional curiosity, so anxious to
make out what it was all about, as perhaps to
lessen his promptitude in action, would scarcely

have been of so much real use as Harry, who had
no *arrière pensée*, but addressed himself to the
immediate emergency with all his might.   He
soothed the sufferer, so that she was soon relieved
by copious floods of tears, which seemed to him
the natural method of getting rid of all that
emotion and excitement, but which surprised
Gilchrist beyond description, and even Miss
Bethune herself, whose complete breakdown was
so unusual and unlike her.   He left her quite at
ease in his mind as to her condition, having persuaded her to lie down, and recommended Gilchrist to darken the room, and keep her mistress
in perfect quiet.

" I will go and look after my things," he said,
"and I'll come back when I have made all my
arrangements, and tell you everything. Oh, don't
speak now! You will be all right in the evening
if you keep quite quiet now : and if you will give
me your advice then, it will be very, very grateful

to me." He made a little warning gesture, keeping her from replying, and then kissed her hand and went away. He had himself pulled down the blind to subdue a little of the garish July daylight, and placed her on a sofa in the corner—ministrations which both mistress and maid permitted with bewilderment, so strange to them was at once the care and the authority of such proceedings. They remained, Miss Bethune on the sofa, Gilchrist, open-mouthed, staring at her, until the door was heard to close upon the young man. Then Miss Bethune rose slowly, with a kind of awe in her face.

"As soon as you think he is out of sight," she said, "Gilchrist, we'll have up the blinds again, but not veesibly, to go against the boy."

"Eh, mem," cried Gilchrist, between laughing and crying, "to bid me darken the room, and you that canna abide the dark, night or day!"

"It was a sweet thought, Gilchrist—all the pure goodness of him and the kind heart."

"I am not saying, mem, but what the young gentleman has a very kind heart."

"You are not saying? And what can you know beyond what's veesible to every person that sees him? It is more than that. Gilchrist, you and all the rest, what do I care what you say? If that is not the voice of nature, what is there to trust to in this whole world? Why should that young lad, bred up so different, knowing nothing of me or my ways, have taken to me? Look at Dora. What a difference! She has no instinct, nothing drawing her to her poor mother. That was a most misfortunate woman, but not an ill woman, Gilchrist. Look how she has done by mine! But Dora has no leaning towards her, no tender thought; whereas he, my bonnie boy —— "

"Mem," said Gilchrist, "but if it was the

voice of nature, it would be double strong in Miss
Dora ; for there is no doubt that it was her mother:
and with this one—oh, my dear leddy, you ken
yoursel' ——"

Miss Bethune gave her faithful servant a look
of flame, and going to the windows, drew up
energetically the blinds, making the springs re-
sound.   Then she said in her most satirical tone :
" And what is it I ken mysel'? "

"Oh, mem," said Gilchrist, " there's a' the evidence, first his ain story, and then the leddy's that
convinced ye for a moment ; and then, what is
most o' a', the old gentleman, the writer, one of
them that kens everything : of the father that died
so many long years ago, and the baby before
him."

Miss Bethune put up her hands to her ears,
she stamped her foot upon the ground. " How
dare ye—how dare ye ? " she cried.   " Either
man or woman that repeats that fool story to me

is no friend of mine. My child, that I've felt in my heart growing up, and seen him boy and man! What's that old man's word—a stranger that knows nothing, that had even forgotten what he was put up to say—in comparison with what is in my heart? Is there such a thing as nature, or no'? Is a mother just like any other person, no better, rather worse? Oh, woman!—you that are a woman! with no call to be rigid about your evidence like a man—what's your evidence to me? I will just tell him when he comes back. 'My bonnie man,' I will say, 'you have been driven here and there in this world, and them that liked you best have failed you; but here is the place where you belong, and here is a love that will never fail!'"

"Oh, my dear leddy, my own mistress," cried Gilchrist, "think—think before you do that! He will ask ye for the evidence, if I am not to ask for it. He's a fine, independent-spirited young gentleman, and he will just shake his head, and say he'll lippen to nobody again. Oh, dinna deceive the young man! Ye might find out after ——"

"What, Gilchrist? Do you think I would change my mind about my own son, and abandon him, like this woman, at the last?"

"I never knew you forsake one that trusted in ye, I'm not saying that; but there might come one after all that had a better claim. There might appear one that even the like of me would believe in—that would have real evidence in his favour, that was no more to be doubted than if he had never been taken away out of your arms."

Miss Bethune turned round quick as lightning upon her maid, her eyes shining, her face full of sudden colour and light. "God bless you, Gilchrist!" she cried, seizing the maid by her shoulders with a half embrace; "I see now you have never believed in that story—no more than me."

Poor Gilchrist could but gape with her mouth open at this unlooked-for turning of the tables. She had presented, without knowing it, the strongest argument of all.

After this, the patient, whom poor Harry had left to the happy influences of quiet and darkness, with all the blinds drawn up and the afternoon sunshine pouring in, went through an hour or two of restless occupation, her mind in the highest activity, her thoughts and her hands full. She promised finally to Gilchrist, not without a mental reservation in the case of special impulse or new light, not to disclose her conviction to Harry, but to wait for at least a day or two on events. But even this resolution did not suffice to reduce her to any condition of quiet, or make the rest which he had prescribed possible. She turned to a number of things

which had been laid aside to be done one time
or another; arrangement of new possessions and
putting away of old, for which previously she
had never found a fit occasion, and despatched
them, scarcely allowing Gilchrist to help her,
at lightning speed.

Finally, she took out an old and heavy jewel-
box, which had stood untouched in her bedroom
for years: for, save an old brooch or two and
some habitual rings which never left her fingers,
Miss Bethune wore no ornaments. She took
them into her sitting-room as the time approached
when Harry might be expected back. It would
give her a countenance, she thought; it would
keep her from fixing her eyes on him while he
spoke, and thus being assailed through all the
armour of the heart at the same time. She could
not look him in the face and see that likeness
which Gilchrist, unconvincible, would not see,
and yet remain silent. Turning over the old-

fashioned jewels, telling him about them, to whom they had belonged, and all the traditions regarding them, would help her in that severe task of self-repression.   She put the box on the table before her, and pulled out the trays.

Nobody in Bloomsbury had seen these treasures before : the box had been kept carefully locked, disguised in an old brown cover, that no one might even guess how valuable it was.   Miss Bethune was almost tempted to send for Dora to see the diamonds in their old-fashioned settings, and that pearl necklace which was still finer in its perfection of lustre and shape.   To call Dora when there was anything to show was so natural, and it might make it easier for her to keep her own counsel ; but she reflected that in Dora's presence the young man would not be more than half hers, and forbore.

Never in her life had those jewels given her so much pleasure.   They had given her no

pleasure, indeed. She had not been allowed to
have them in that far-off stormy youth, which had
been lightened by such a sweet, guilty gleam of
happiness, and quenched in such misery of downfall. When they came to her by inheritance, like
all the rest, these beautiful things had made her
heart sick. What could she do with them—a
woman whose life no longer contained any possible
festival, who had nobody coming after her, no heir
to make heirlooms sweet? She had locked the
box, and almost thrown away the key, which,
however, was a passionate suggestion repugnant
to common sense, and resolved itself naturally
into confiding the key to Gilchrist, in whose most
secret repositories it had been kept, with an
occasional furtive interval during which the maid
had secretly visited and "polished up" the jewels,
making sure that they were all right. Neither
mistress nor maid was quite aware of their value,
and both probably exaggerated it in their thoughts ;

but some of the diamonds were fine, though all were very old-fashioned in arrangement, and the pearls were noted. Miss Bethune pulled out the trays, and the gems flashed and sparkled in a thousand colours in the slant of sunshine which poured in its last level ray through one window, just before the sun set—and made a dazzling show upon the table, almost blinding Janie, who came up with a message, and could not restrain a little shriek of wonder and admiration. The letter was one of trouble and appeal from poor Mrs. Hesketh, who and her husband were becoming more and more a burden on the shoulders of their friends. It asked for money, as usual, just a little money to go on with, as the shop in which they had been set up was not as yet producing much. The letter had been written with evident reluctance, and was marked with blots of tears. Miss Bethune's mind was too much excited to consider calmly any such petition. Full herself

of anticipation, of passionate hope, and visionary
enthusiasm, which transported her above all
common things, how was she to refuse a poor
woman's appeal for the bare necessities of
existence—a woman "near her trouble," with
a useless husband, who was unworthy, yet whom
the poor soul loved? She called Gilchrist, who
generally carried the purse, to get something for
the poor little pair.

"Is there anybody waiting?" she asked.

"Oh ay, mem," said Gilchrist, "there's
somebody waiting, — just him himsel', the
weirdless creature, that is good for nothing."
Gilchrist did not approve of all her mistress's
liberalities. "I would not just be their milch
cow to give them whatever they're wanting,"
she said. "It's awful bad for any person to
just know where to run when they are in any
trouble."

"Hold your peace!" cried her mistress.

"Am I one to shut up my heart when the bless-ing of God has come to me?"

"Oh, mem!" cried Gilchrist, remonstrating, holding up her hands.

But Miss Bethune stamped her foot, and the wiser woman yielded.

She found Hesketh standing at the door of the sitting-room, when she went out to give him, very unwillingly, the money for his wife. "The impident weirdless creature! He would have been in upon my leddy in another moment, press-ing to her very presence with his impident ways!" cried Gilchrist, hot and indignant. The faithful woman paused at the door as she came back, and looked at her mistress turning over and rearranging these treasures. "And her sitting playing with her bonnie dies, in a rapture like a little bairn!" she said to herself, putting up her apron to her eyes. And then Gilchrist shook her head—shook it, growing quicker and quicker in

the movement, as if she would have twisted
it off.

But Miss Bethune was "very composed"
when young Gordon came back. With an
intense sense of the humour of the position,
which mistress and maid communicated to each
other with one glance of tacit co-operation,
these two women comported themselves as if
the behests of the young visitor who had
taken the management of Miss Bethune's
accés des nerfs upon himself, had been carried
out. She assumed, almost unconsciously, notwithstanding the twinkle in her eye, the languid
aspect of a woman who has been resting after
unusual excitement. All women, they say (as
they say so many foolish things), are actors ; all
women, at all events, let us allow, learn as the
A B C of their training the art of taking up a rôle
assigned to them, and fulfilling the necessities of a
position. "You will see what I'm reduced to by

what I'm doing," she said. "As if there was
nothing of more importance in life, I am just
playing myself with my toys, like Dora, or any
other little thing."

"So much the best thing you could do," said
young Harry; and he was eager and delighted
to look through the contents of the box with
her.

He was far better acquainted with their value
than she was, and while she told him the family
associations connected with each ornament, he
discussed very learnedly what they were, and
distinguished the old-fashioned rose diamonds
which were amongst those of greater value,
with a knowledge that seemed to her extraordinary. They spent, in fact, an hour easily
and happily over that box, quite relieved from
graver considerations by the interposition of a
new thing, in which there were no deep secrets
of the heart or commotions of being involved:

and thus were brought down into the ordinary
from the high and troublous level of feeling
and excitement on which they had been. To
Miss Bethune the little episode was one of
child's play in the midst of the most serious
questions of the world. Had she thought it
possible beforehand that such an interval could
have been, she would, in all likelihood, have
scorned herself for the dereliction, and almost
scorned the young man for being able to forget
at once his sorrow and the gravity of his circumstances at sight of anything so trifling
as a collection of trinkets. But in reality this
interlude was balm to them both. It revealed to
Miss Bethune a possibility of ordinary life and
intercourse, made sweet by understanding and
affection, which was a revelation to her repressed
and passionate spirit; and it soothed the youth
with that renewing of fresh interests, reviving and
succeeding the old, which gives elasticity to the

mind, and courage to face the world anew. They did not know how long they had been occupied over the jewels, when the hour of dinner came round again, and Gilchrist appeared with her preparations, still further increasing that sense of peaceful life renewed, and the order of common things begun again. It was only after this meal was over, the jewels being all restored to their places, and the box to its old brown cover in Miss Bethune's bedroom, that the discussion of the graver question was resumed.

"There is one thing," Miss Bethune said, "that, however proud you may be, you must let me say: and that is, that everything having turned out so different to your thoughts, and you left—you will not be offended?—astray, as it were, in this big unfriendly place ——"

"I cannot call it unfriendly," said young Gordon. "If other people find it so, it is not my experience. I have found you." He looked up at her with a half laugh, with moisture in his eyes.

"Ay," she said, with emphasis, "you have found me—you say well—found me when you were not looking for me. I accept the word as a good omen. And after that?"

If only she would not have abashed him from time to time with those dark sayings, which seemed to mean something to which he had no clue! He felt himself brought suddenly to a standstill in his grateful effusion of feeling, and put up his hand to arrest her in what she was evidently going on to say.

"Apart from that," he said hurriedly, "I am not penniless. I have not been altogether dependent; at least, the form of my dependence has been the easiest one. I have had my allowance from my guardian ever since I came to man's estate. It was my own, though, of course, of his giving. And I am not an extravagant fellow. It was not as if I wanted money for to-morrow's living, for daily bread." He coloured as he spoke, with the half pride, half shame, of discussing such a subject. "I think," he said, throwing off that flush with a shake of his head, "that I have enough to take me back to South America, and there, I told you, I have friends. I don't think I can fail to find work there."

" But under such different circumstances! Have you considered? A poor clerk where you were one of the fine gentlemen of the place. Such a change of position is easier where you are not known."

He grew red again, with a more painful colour. "I don't think so," he said quickly. "I don't believe that my old friends would cast me off because, instead of being a useless fellow about town, I was a poor clerk."

"Maybe you are right," said Miss Bethune very gravely. "I am not one that thinks so ill of human nature. They would not cast you off. But you, working hard all day, wearied at night, with no house to entertain them in that entertained you, would it not be you that would cast off them?"

He looked at her, startled, for a moment. "Do you think," he cried, "that poverty makes a man mean like that?" And then he added slowly : "It is possible, perhaps, that it might be so". Then he brightened up again, and looked her full in the face. "But then there would be nobody to blame for that, it would be simply my own fault."

"God bless you, laddie!" cried Miss Bethune quite irrelevantly ; and then she too paused. "If it should happen so that there was a place provided for you at home. No, no, not what you call dependence—far from it, hard work. I know

one—a lady that has property in the North—
property that has not been well managed—that
has given her more trouble than it is worth. But
there's much to be made of it, if she had a man
who would give his mind to it as if—as if it were
his own."

"But I," he said, "know nothing about the
North. I would not know how to manage. I
told you I had no education. And would this
lady have me, trust me, put that in my hands,
without knowing, without ——"

"She would trust you," said Miss Bethune,
clasping her hands together firmly, and looking
him in the face, in a rigid position which showed
how little steady she was—"she would trust you,
for life and death, on my word."

His eyes fell before that unfathomable concen-
tration of hers. "And you would trust me like
that—knowing so little, so little? And how can
you tell even that I am honest—even that I am

true? That there's nothing behind, no weakness, no failure?"

"Don't speak to me," she said harshly. "I know."

CHAPTER XXII.

THE evening passed, however, without any further revelations. Miss Bethune explained to the young man, with all the lucidity of a man of business, the situation and requirements of that "property in the North," which would give returns, she believed, of various kinds, not always calculated in balance sheets, if it was looked after by a man who would deal with it "as if it were his own". The return would be something in money and rents, but much more in human comfort and happiness. She had never had the courage to tackle that problem, she said, and the place had been terrible to her, full of associations which would be thought of no more if he were there. The result was, that young Gordon went away thoughtful, somewhat touched by the feeling with which

Miss Bethune had spoken of her poor crofters, somewhat roused by the thought of "the North," that vague and unknown country which was the country of his fathers, the land of brown heath and shaggy wood, the country of Scott, which is, after all, distinction enough for any well-conditioned stranger. Should he try that strange new opening of life suddenly put before him? The unknown of itself has a charm—

> If the pass were dangerous known,
> The danger's self were lure alone.

He went back to his hotel with at least a new project fully occupying all his thoughts.

On the next evening, in the dusk of the summer night, Miss Bethune was in her bed-chamber alone. She had no light, though she was a lover of the light, and had drawn up the blinds as soon as the young physician who prescribed a darkened room had disappeared. She had a habit of watching out the last departing rays of daylight, and loved to sit in the gloaming, as she called it, reposing from all the cares of the day in that meditative moment. It was a bad sign of Miss Bethune's state of mind when she called early for her lamp. She was seated thus in the dark, when young Gordon came in audibly to the sitting-room, introduced by Gilchrist, who told him her mistress would be with him directly ; but, knowing Miss Bethune would hear what she said, did not come to call her. The lamps were lighted in that room, and showed a little outline of light through the chinks of the door. She smiled to herself in the dark, with a beatitude that ought to have lighted it up, as she listened to the big movements of the young man in the lighted room next door. He had seated himself under Gilchrist's ministrations ; but when she went away he got up and moved about, looking, as Miss Bethune divined, at the pictures on the walls and the books and little silver toys on the tables.

He made more noise, she thought to herself proudly, than a woman does: filled the space more, seemed to occupy and fill out everything. Her countenance and her heart expanded in the dark; she would have liked to peep at him through the crevice of light round the door, or even the keyhole, to see him when he did not know she was looking, to read the secrets of his heart in his face. There were none there, she said to herself with an effusion of happiness which brought the tears to her eyes, none there which a mother should be afraid to discover. The luxury of sitting there, holding her breath, hearing him move, knowing him so near, was so sweet and so great, that she sat, too blessed to move, taking all the good out of that happy moment before it should fleet away.

Suddenly, however, there came a dead silence. Had he sat down again? Had he gone out on the balcony? What had become of him? She sat breathless, wondering, listening for the next sound. Surely he had stepped outside the window to look out upon the Bloomsbury street, and the waving of the trees in the Square, and the stars shining overhead. Not a sound—yet, yes, there was something. What was it? A faint, stealthy rustling, not to be called a sound at all, rather some stealthy movement to annihilate sound— the strangest contrast to the light firm step that had come into the room, and the free movements which she had felt to be bigger than a woman's.

Miss Bethune in the dark held her breath; fear seized possession of her, she knew not why; her heart sank, she knew not why. Oh, his father —his father was not a good man!

The rustling continued, very faint; it might have been a small animal rubbing against the door. She sat bolt upright in her chair, motion-less, silent as a waxen image, listening. If perhaps, after all, it should be only one of the little girls, or even the cat rubbing against the wall idly on the way downstairs! A troubled smile came over her face, her heart gave a throb of relief. But then the sound changed, and Miss Bethune's face again grew rigid, her heart stood still.

Some one was trying very cautiously, without noise, to open the door; to turn the handle without making any sound required some time; it creaked a little, and then there was silence—guilty silence, the pause of stealth alarmed by the faintest noise: then it began again. Slowly, slowly the handle turned round, the door opened, a hair's breadth at a time. O Lord above! his father— his father was an ill man.

There was some one with her in the room— some one unseen, as she was, swallowed up in the darkness, veiled by the curtains at the windows, which showed faintly a pale streak of

sky only, letting in no light.   Unseen, but not
inaudible ; a hurried, fluttering breath betraying
him, and that faint sound of cautious, uneasy
movement, now and then instantly, guiltily
silenced, and then resumed.   She could feel the
stealthy step thrill the flooring, making a jar,
which was followed by one of those complete
silences in which the intruder too held his breath,
then another stealthy step.

A thousand thoughts, a very avalanche, pre-
cipitated themselves through her mind.   A man
did not steal into a dark room like that if he were
doing it for the first time.   And his words last
night, " How do you know even that I am honest?"
And then his father—his father—oh, God help
him, God forgive him !—that was an ill man !
And his upbringing in a country where lies were
common, with a guardian that did him no justice,
and the woman that cut him off.   And not to
know that he had a creature belonging to him in

the world to be made glad or sorry whatever happened! Oh, God forgive him, God help him! the unfortunate, the miserable boy! "Mine all the same—-mine all the same!" her heart said, bleeding—oh, that was no metaphor! bleeding with the anguish, the awful, immeasurable blow.

If there was any light at all in the room, it was a faint greyness, just showing in the midst of the dark the vague form of a little table against the wall, and a box in a brown cover—-a box—no, no, the shape of a box, but only something standing there, something, the accursed thing for which life and love were to be wrecked once more. Oh, his father—his father! But his father would not have done that. Yet it was honester to take the trinkets, the miserable stones that would bring in money, than to wring a woman's heart. And what did the boy know? He had never been taught, never had any example, God help him, God forgive him! and mine—mine all the time!

Then out of the complete darkness came into that faint grey where the box was, an arm, a hand. It touched, not calculating the distance, the solid substance with a faint jar, and retired like a ghost, while she sat rigid, looking on ; then more cautiously, more slowly still, it stole forth again, and grasped the box. Miss Bethune had settled nothing what to do, she had thought of nothing but the misery of it, she had intended, so far as she had any intention, to watch while the tragedy was played out, the dreadful act accomplished. But she was a woman of sudden impulses, moved by flashes of resolution almost independent of her will.

Suddenly, more ghostlike still than the arm of the thief, she made a swift movement forward, and put her hand upon his. Her grasp seemed to crush through the quivering clammy fingers, and she felt under her own the leap of the pulses ; but the criminal was prepared for every emergency, and uttered no cry. She felt the quick noiseless change of attitude, and then the free arm swing to strike her—heaven and earth! to strike her, a woman twice his age, to strike her, his friend, his —— She was a strong woman, in the fulness of health and courage. As quick as lightning, she seized the arm as it descended, and held him as in a grip of iron. Was it guilt that made him like a child in her hold? He had a stick in his hand, shortened, with a heavy head, ready to deal a blow. Oh, the coward, the wretched coward! She held him panting for a moment, unable to say a word; and then she called out with a voice that was no vóice, but a kind of roar of misery, for "Gilchrist, Gilchrist!"

Gilchrist, who was never far off, who always had her ear open for her mistress, heard, and came flying from up or down stairs with her candle: and some one else heard it, who was

standing pensive on the balcony, looking out, and
wondering what fate had now in store for him,
and mingling his thoughts with the waving of
the trees and the nameless noises of the street.
Which of them arrived first was never known, he
from the other room throwing wide the door of
communication, or she from the stairs with the
impish, malicious light of that candle throwing in
its sudden illumination as with a pleasure in the
deed.

The spectators were startled beyond measure
to see the lady in apparent conflict with a man,
but they had no time to make any remarks. The
moment the light flashed upon her, Miss Bethune
gave a great cry. " It's you, ye vermin !" she
cried, flinging the furtive creature in her grasp
from her against the wall, which half stunned him
for the moment. And then she stood for a
moment, her head bent back, her face without a
trace of colour, confronting the eager figure in

the doorway, surrounded by the glow of the light, flying forward to help her.

"O God, forgive me!" she cried, "God, forgive me, for I am an ill woman: but I will never forgive myself!"

The man who lay against the wall, having dropped there on the floor with the vehemence of her action, perhaps exaggerating the force that had been used against him, to excite pity—for Gilchrist, no mean opponent, held one door, and that unexpected dreadful apparition of the young man out of the lighted room bearing down upon him, filled the other—was Alfred Hesketh, white, miserable, and cowardly, huddled up in a wretched heap, with furtive eyes gleaming, and the heavy-headed stick furtively grasped, still ready to deal an unexpected blow, had he the opportunity, though he was at the same-time rubbing the wrist that held it, as if in pain.

Young Gordon had made a hurried step

towards him, when Miss Bethune put out her hand. She had dropped into a chair, where she sat panting for breath.

"Wait," she said, "wait till I can speak."

"You brute!" cried Harry; "how dare you come in here? What have you done to frighten the lady?"

He was interrupted by a strange chuckle of a laugh from Miss Bethune's panting throat.

"It's rather me, I'm thinking, that's frightened him," she said. "Ye wretched vermin of a creature, how did ye know? What told ye in your meeserable mind that there was something here to steal? And ye would have struck me—me that am dealing out to ye your daily bread! No, my dear, you're not to touch him; don't lay a finger on him. The Lord be thanked—though God forgive me for thanking Him for the wickedness of any man!"

How enigmatical this all was to Harry Gordon, and how little he could imagine any clue to the mystery, it is needless to say. Gilchrist herself thought her mistress was temporarily out of her mind. She was quicker, however, to realise what had happened than the young man, who did not think of the jewels, nor remember anything about them. Gilchrist looked with anxiety at her lady's white face and gleaming eyes.

"Take her into the parlour, Master Harry," she said : "she's just done out. And I'll send for the police."

"You'll do nothing of the kind, Gilchrist," said Miss Bethune. "Get up, ye creature. You're not worth either man's or woman's while ; you have no more fusion than a cat. Get up, and begone, ye poor, weak, wretched, cowardly vermin, for that's what ye are : and I thank the Lord with all my heart that it was only you!

Gilchrist, stand away from the door, and let the creature go."

He rose, dragging himself up by degrees, with a furtive look at Gordon, who, indeed, looked a still less easy opponent than Miss Bethune.

" I take that gentleman to witness," he said, "as there's no evidence against me but just a lady's fancy : and I've been treated very bad, and my wrist broken, for aught I know, and bruised all over, and I ——"

Miss Bethune stamped her foot on the floor. "Begone, ye born liar and robber!" she said. " Gilchrist will see ye off the premises ; and mind, you never come within my sight again. Now, Mr. Harry, as she calls ye, I'll go into the parlour, as she says ; and the Lord, that only knows the wickedness that has been in my mind, forgive me this night! and it would be a comfort to my heart, my bonnie man, if you would say Amen."

"Amen with all my heart," said the young man, with a smile, "but, so far as I can make out, your wickedness is to be far too good and forgiving. What did the fellow do? I confess I should not like to be called a vermin, as you called him freely—but if he came with intent to steal he should have been handed over to the police, indeed he should."

" I am more worthy of the police than him, if ye but knew : but heaven be praised you'll never know. I mind now, he came with a message when I was playing with these wretched diamonds, like an old fool : and he must have seen or scented them with the creeminal instinct Dr. Roland speaks about."

She drew a long breath, for she had not yet recovered from the panting of excitement, and then told her story, the rustling without, the opening of the door, the hand extended to the box. When she had told all this with much vividness, Miss Bethune suddenly stopped, drew another long breath, and dropped back upon the sofa where she was sitting. It was not her way ; the lights had been dazzling and confusing her ever since they blazed upon her by the opening of the two doors, and the overwhelming horror, and blessed but tremendous revulsion of feeling, which had passed in succession over her, had been more than her strength, already undermined by excitement, could bear. Her breath, her consciousness, her life, seemed to ebb away in a moment, leaving only a pale shadow of her, fallen back upon the cushions.

Once more Harry was the master of the situation. He had seen a woman faint before, which was almost more than Gilchrist with all her experience had done, and he had the usual remedies at his fingers' ends. But this was not like the usual easy faints, over in a minute, to which young Gordon had been accustomed, and Dr. Roland

had to be summoned from below, and a thrill of
alarm had run through the house, Mrs. Simcox
herself coming up from the kitchen, with strong
salts and feathers to burn, before Miss Bethune
came to herself. The house was frightened, and
so at last was the experienced Harry; but Dr.
Roland's interest and excitement may be said to
have been pleasurable. " I have always thought
this was what was likely. I've been prepared for
it," he said to himself, as he hovered round the
sofa. It would be wrong to suppose that he
lengthened, or at least did nothing to shorten, this
faint for his own base purposes, that he might the
better make out certain signs which he thought
he had recognised. But the fact was, that not
only Dora had come from abovestairs, but even
Mr. Mannering had dragged himself down, on
the alarm that Miss Bethune was dead or dying;
and that the whole household had gathered in her
room, or on the landing outside; while she lay,

in complicity (or not) with the doctor, in that long-continued swoon, which the spectators afterwards said lasted an hour, or two, or even three hours, according to their temperaments.

When she came to herself at last, the scene upon which she opened her eyes was one which helped her recovery greatly, by filling her with wrath and indignation. She lay in the middle of her room, in a strong draught, the night air blowing from window to window across her, the lamp even under its shade, much more the candles on the mantelpiece, blown about, and throwing a wavering glare upon the agitated group, Gilchrist in the foreground with her apron at her eyes, and behind her Dora, red with restrained emotions, and Janie and Molly crying freely, while Mrs. Simcox brandished a bunch of fuming feathers, and Mr. Mannering peered over the landlady's head with his "pince-nez" insecurely balanced on his nose, and his legs trembling under him in

a harmony of unsteadiness, but anxiety. Miss
Bethune's wrist was in the grasp of the doctor ;
and Harry stood behind with a fan, which, in the
strong wind blowing across her from window to
window, struck the patient as ludicrously unnecessary. " What is all this fuss about ? " she
cried, trying to raise herself up.

" There's no fuss, my dear lady," said the
doctor ; " but you must keep perfectly quiet."

" Oh, you're there, Dr. Roland ? Then there's
one sane person. But for goodness' sake make
Mr. Mannering sit down, and send all these idiots
away. What's the matter with me, that I've to
get my death of cold, and be murdered with that
awful smell, and even Harry Gordon behaving
like a fool, making an air with a fan, when there's
a gale blowing ? Go away, go away."

" You see that our friend has come to herself,"
said the doctor. " Shut that window, somebody,
the other will be enough ; and, my dear woman,

for the sake of all that's good, take those horrid feathers away."

"I am murdered with the smell!" cried Miss Bethune, placing her hands over her face. "But make Mr. Mannering sit down, he's not fit to stand after his illness ; and Harry, boy, sit down, too, and don't drive me out of my senses. Go away, go all of you away."

The last to be got rid of was Dr. Roland, who assured everybody that the patient was now quite well, but languid. "You want to get rid of me too, I know," he said, "and I'm going ; but I should like to see you in bed first."

"You shall not see me in bed, nor no other man," said Miss Bethune. "I will go to bed when I am disposed, doctor. I'm not your patient, mind, at all events, now."

"You were half an hour since : but I'm not going to pretend to any authority," said the doctor. "I hope I know better. Don't agitate yourself any more, if you'll be guided by me. You have been screwing up that heart of yours far too tight."

" How do you know," she said, " that I have got a heart at all ? "

" Probably not from the sentimental point of view," he replied, with a little fling of sarcasm : " but I know you couldn't live without the physical organ, and it's over-strained. Good-night, since I see you want to get rid of me. But I'll be handy downstairs, and mind you come for me, Gilchrist, on the moment if she should show any signs again."

This was said to Gilchrist in an undertone as the doctor went away.

Miss Bethune sat up on her sofa, still very pale, still with a singing in her ears, and the glitter of fever in her eyes. " You are not to go away, Harry," she said. " I have something to tell you before you go."

"Oh, mem," said Gilchrist, "for any sake, not to-night."

"Go away, and bide away till I send for you," cried the mistress. "And, Harry, sit you down here by me. I am going to tell you a story. This night has taught me many things. I might die, or I might be murdered for the sake of a few gewgaws that are nothing to me and go down to my grave with a burden on my heart. I want to speak before I die."

"Not to-night," he cried. "You are in no danger. I'll sleep here on the sofa by way of guard, and to-morrow you will send them to your bankers. Don't tire yourself any more to-night."

"You are like all the rest, and understand nothing about it," she cried impatiently. "It is just precisely now that I will speak, and no other time. Harry, I am going to tell you a story. It is like most women's stories—about a young creature that was beguiled and loved a man. He

was a man that had a fine outside, and looked as
good as he was bonnie, or at least this misfortunate thing thought so. He had nothing, and she
had nothing. But she was the last of her family,
and would come into a good fortune if she pleased
her uncle that was the head of the name. But
the uncle could not abide this man. Are you
listening to me? Mind, it is a story, but not an
idle story, and every word tells. Well, she was
sent away to a lonely country place, an old
house, with two old servants in it, to keep
her free of the man. But the man followed;
and in that solitude who was to hinder them
seeing each other? They did for a while
every day. And then the two married each
other, as two can do in Scotland that make up
their minds to risk it, and were living together in
secret in the depths of the Highlands, as I told
you, nobody knowing but the old servants that
had been far fonder of her father than of the uncle

that was head of the house, and were faithful to her in life and death. And then there came terrible news that the master was coming back. That poor young woman—oh, she was a fool, and I do not defend her!—had just been delivered in secret, in trouble and misery—for she dared not seek help or nursing but what she got at home— of a bonnie bairn,"—she put out her hand and grasped him by the arm,—"a boy, a darling, though she had him but for two or three days. Think if you can what that was. The master coming that had, so to speak, the power of life and death in his hands, and the young, subdued girl that he had put there to be in safety, the mother of a son ——" Miss Bethune drew a long breath. She silenced the remonstrance on the lips of her hearer by a gesture, and went on :—

" It was the man, her husband, that she thought loved her, that brought the news. He said everything was lost if it should be known. He bid her to be brave and put a good face upon it, for his sake and the boy's. Keep her fortune and cling to her inheritance she must, whatever happened, for their sake. And while she was dazed in her weakness, and could not tell what to think, he took the baby out of her arms, and carried him away.

" Harry Gordon, that's five and twenty years ago, and man or bairn I have never seen since, though I did that for them. I dreed my weird for ten long years—ten years of mortal trouble— and never said a word, and nobody knew. Then my uncle died, and the money, the terrible money, bought with my life's blood, became mine. And I looked for him then to come back. But he never came back nor word nor sign of him. And my son--the father, I had discovered what he was, I wanted never to hear his name again—but my son—Harry Gordon, that's you! They may say what they will, but I know better. Who should know, if not the mother that bore you? My heart went out to you when I saw you first, and yours to me. You'll not tell me that your heart did not speak for your mother? It is you, my darling, it is you!"

He had staggered to his feet, pale, trembling, and awe-stricken. The sight of her emotion, the pity of her story, the revolt and resistance in his own heart were too much for him. "I!" he cried.

CHAPTER XXIII.

Harry Gordon passed the night upon the sofa in Miss Bethune's sitting-room. It was his opinion that her nerves were so shaken and her mind so agitated that the consciousness of having some one at hand within call, in case of anything happening, was of the utmost consequence. I don't know that any one else in the house entertained these sentiments, but it was an idea in which he could not be shaken, his experience all tending in that way.

As a matter of fact, his nerves were scarcely less shaken than he imagined hers to be. His mother! Was that his mother who called good-night to him from the next room? who held that amusing colloquy with the doctor through the closed door, defying all interference, and bidding

Dr. Roland look after his patient upstairs, and leave her in peace with Gilchrist, who was better than any doctor? Was that his mother? His heart beat with a strange confusion, but made no answer. And his thoughts went over all the details with an involuntary scepticism. No, there was no voice of nature, as she had fondly hoped ; nothing but the merest response to kind words and a kind look had drawn him towards this old Scotch maiden lady, who he had thought, with a smile, reminded him of something in Scott, and therefore had an attraction such as belongs to those whom we may have known in some previous state of being.

What a strange fate was his, to be drawn into one circle after another, one family after another, to which he had no right! And how was he to convince this lady, who was so determined in her own way of thinking, that he had no right, no title, to consider himself her son ? But had he indeed no title? Was she likely to make such a statement without proof that it was true, without evidence? He thought of her with a kind of amused but by no means disrespectful admiration, as she had stood flinging from her the miserable would-be thief, the wretched, furtive creature who was no match for a resolute and dauntless woman. All the women Harry had ever known would have screamed or fled or fainted at sight of a live burglar in their very bed-chamber. She flung him off like a fly, like a reptile. That was not a weak woman, liable to be deceived by any fancy. She had the look in her eyes of a human creature afraid of nothing, ready to confront any danger. And could she then be so easily deceived? Or was it true, actually true? Was he the son—not of a woman whom it might be shame to discover, as he had always feared—but of a spotless mother, a person of note, with an established position and secure fortune? The land which he was to manage, which she had roused him almost to enthusiasm about, by her talk of crofters and cotters to be helped forward, and human service to be done—was that land his own, coming to him by right, his natural place and inheritance? Was he no waif and stray, no vague atom in the world drifting hither and thither, but a man with an assured position, a certain home, a place in society? How different from going back to South America, and at the best becoming a laborious clerk where he had been the young master! But he could not believe in it.

He lay there silent through the short summer night, moving with precaution upon the uneasy couch, which was too short and too small, but where the good fellow would have passed the night waking and dosing for anybody's comfort, even were it only an old woman's who had been kind to him. But was she his mother—his mother? He could not believe it—he could not, he could not! Her wonderful speeches and looks were all explained now, and went to his heart: but they did not convince him, or bring any enlightenment into his. Was she the victim of an illusion, poor lady, self-deceived altogether? Or was there something in it, or was there nothing in it? He thought of his father, and his heart revolted. His poor father, whom he remembered with the halo round him of childish affection, but whom he had learned to see through other people's eyes, not a strong man, not good for very much, but yet not one to desert a woman who trusted in him. But of the young man's thoughts through that long uneasy night there was no end. He heard whisperings and movements in the next room, subdued for his sake as he subdued his inclination to turn and toss upon his sofa for hers, during half the night. And then when the daylight came bright into the room through the bars of the venetian blind there came silence, just when he had fully woke up to the consciousness that life had begun again in a new world. A little later, Gilchrist stole into his room, bringing him a cup of tea. "You must come upstairs now; there's a room where ye will get some sleep. She's sound now, and it's broad daylight, and no fear of any disturbance," she said.

"I want no more sleep. I'll go and get a bath, and be ready for whatever is wanted." He caught her apron as she was turning away, that apron on which so many hems had been folded. "Don't go away," he said. "Speak to me, tell me, Gilchrist, for heaven's sake, is this true?"

"The Lord knows!" cried Gilchrist, shaking her head and clasping her hands; "but oh, my young gentleman, dinna ask me!"

"Whom can I ask?" he said. "Surely, surely you, that have been always with her, can throw some light upon it. Is it true?"

"It is true—true as death," said the woman,

" that all that has happened to my dear leddy; but oh, if you are the bairn, the Lord knows ; he was but two days old, and he would have been about your age. I can say not a word, but only the Lord knows. And there's nothing—nothing, though she thinks sae, that speaks in your heart ? "

He shook his head, with a faint smile upon his face.

"Oh, dinna laugh, dinna laugh. I canna bear it, Mr. Harry ; true or no' true, it's woven in with every fibre o' her heart. You have nae parents, my bonnie man. Oh, could you no' take it upon ye, true or no' true ? There's naebody I can hear of that it would harm or wrong if you were to accept it. And there's naebody kens but me how good she is. Her exterior is maybe no' sae smooth as many ; but her heart it is gold—oh, her heart it is gold ! For God's sake, who is the Father of all of us, and full of mercy—such peety as a father hath unto his children dear—oh, my young man, let her believe it, take her at her word! You will make her a happy woman at the end of a' her trouble, and it will do ye nae harm."

"Not if it is a fiction all the time," he said, shaking his head.

"Who is to prove it's a fiction? He would have been your age. She thinks you have your grandfather's een. I'm no' sure now I look at you but she's right. She's far more likely to be right than me: and now I look at you well I think I can see it. Oh, Mr. Harry, what harm would it do you? A good home and a good inheritance, and to make her happy. Is that no' worth while, even if maybe it were not what you would think perfitly true?"

"It can't be half true, Gilchrist; it must be whole or nothing."

"Weel, then, it's whole true; and I'll gang

to the stake for it. Is she not the one that should know ? And if you were to cast her off the morn and break her heart, she would still believe it till her dying day. Turn round your head and let me look at you again. Oh, laddie, if I were to gang to the stake for it, you have—you have your grandfather's een ! "

CHAPTER XXIV.

The house in Bloomsbury was profoundly agitated by all these discoveries. Curiously enough, and against all the previsions of his friends, Mr. Mannering had not been thrown back by the excitement. The sharp sting of these events which had brought back before him once more the tragic climax of his life—the time when he had come back as out of the grave and found his home desolate—when his wife had fled before his face, not daring to meet his eye, although she had not knowingly sinned against him, and when all the triumph of his return to life, and of his discoveries and the fruit of his dreadful labours, had become bitterness to him and misery—came back upon him, every incident standing out as if it had been yesterday. He had fallen into the dead calm of failure, he had dropped his tools from his hands, and all his ambition from his heart. He had retired—he who had reappeared in existence after all his sufferings, with the consciousness that now the ball was at his foot, and fame if not fortune secured—into the second desert, more impenetrable than any African forest, of these rooms in Bloomsbury, and vegetated there all these years, forgetting more or less all that had happened to him, and all that might have happened to him, and desiring only to linger out the last of his life unknowing and unknown. And now into his calm there had come back, clear as yesterday, all that terrible climax, every detail of his own tragedy.

It ought to have killed him : that would have seemed the most likely event in his weakness, after his long illness ; and perhaps,—who could say?—the best thing that could have happened, in face of the new circumstances, which he could not accept and had no right to refuse. But no, it did not kill him. It acted upon him as great trouble acts on some minds, like a strong stimulant. It stung him back into life, it seemed to transfuse something, some new revivifying principle, into his veins. He had wanted, perhaps, something to disperse the mists of illness and physical dejection. He found it not in soothing influences or pleasure, but in pain. From the day when he stumbled downstairs to Miss Bethune's room on the dreadful report that she was dying, he began at once to resume his usual habits, and with almost more than his usual strength. Was it possible that Death, that healer of all wounds, that peacemaker in all tumults, had restored a rest that was wanting to the man's secret heart, never disclosed to any ear? She was dead, the woman who unwittingly, without meaning it, had made of his life the silent tragedy it had been. That she was guiltless, and that the catastrophe was all a terrible mistake, had made it worse instead of better. He had thought often that had she erred in passion, had she been carried away from him by some strong gale of personal feeling, it would have been more bearable: but the cruel fatality, the network of accident which had made his life desolate, and hers he knew not what—this was what was intolerable, a thing not to bear thinking of.

But now she was dead, all the misery over, nothing left but the silence. She had been nothing to him for years, torn out of his heart, flung out of his life, perhaps with too little pity, perhaps with little perception of the great sacrifice she had made in giving up to him without even a protest her only child : but her very existence had been a canker in his life ; the thought that still the same circle of earth enclosed them— him and the woman who had once been everything to him, and then nothing, yet always something, something, a consciousness, a fever, a jarring note that set all life out of tune. And now she was dead. The strong pain of all this revival stung him back to strength. He went out in defiance of the doctor, back to his usual work, resuming the daily round. He had much to meet, to settle, to set right again, in his renewed exist-ence. And she was dead. The other side of life was closed and sealed, and the stone rolled to the door of the sepulchre. Nothing could happen to bring that back, to renew any consciousness of it more. Strange and sad and disturbing as this event was, it seemed to settle and clear the turbid current of a spoiled life.

And perhaps the other excitement and climax of the life of his neighbour which had been going on under the same roof, helped Mr. Mannering in the renewal of his own history. When he heard Miss Bethune's story, the silent rebellion against his own, which had been ever in his mind, was silenced. It is hard, in the comparison of

troubles, which people who have been more or
less crushed in life are so fond of making, when
brought into sufficiently intimate relation with
each other, to have to acknowledge that perhaps
a brother pilgrim, a sister, has had more to bear
than oneself. Even in misery we love to be
foremost, to have the bitter in our cup acknow-
ledged as more bitter than that of others.
But yet, when Mr. Mannering heard, as she
could tell him, the story of the woman who had
lived so near him for years with that unsuspected
secret, he did not deny that her lot had been
more terrible than his own. Miss Bethune was
eager to communicate her own tale in those days
of excitement and transition. She went to him
of her own accord after the first day of his return to his work, while the doctor hovered about
the stairs, up and down, and could not rest, in
terror for the result. Dr. Roland could not believe that his patient would not break down. He

could not go out, nor even sit quietly in his own room, lest he should be wanted, and not ready at the first call.   He could not refrain from a gibe at the lady he met on the stairs.   "Yes, by all means," he said, "go and tell him all about your own business.   Go and send him out to look after that wretched Hesketh, whom you are going to keep up, I hear, all the same."

"Not him, doctor.   The poor unhappy young creature, his wife."

"Oh, yes ; that is how these miserable villains get hold upon people of weak minds.   His wife! I'd have sent him to gaol.   His wife would have been far better without a low blackguard like that. But don't let me keep you.   Go and give the *coup de grace* to Mannering.   I shall be ready, whatever happens, downstairs."

But Miss Bethune did not give Mannering the *coup de grace.*   On the contrary, she helped forward the cure which the climax of his own per-

sonal tragedy had begun. It gave both these
people a kind of forlorn pleasure to think that
there was a kind of resemblance in their fate, and
that they had lived so long beside each other
without knowing it, without suspecting how unlike other people their respective lives had been.
The thought of the unhappy young woman, whose
husband of a year and whose child of a day had
been torn from her, who had learnt so sadly to
know the unworthiness of the one, and whose
heart and imagination had for five and twenty
years dwelt upon the other, without any possible
outlet, and with a hope which she had herself
known to be fantastic and without hope, filled
Mannering with a certain awe. He had suffered
for little more than half that time, and he had not
been deprived of his Dora. He began to think
pitifully, even mercifully, of the woman who had
left him that one alleviation in his life.

"I bow my head before her," Miss Bethune

said. " She must have been a just woman.   The
bairn was yours, and she had no right to take her
from you.   She fled before your appearance, she
could not look you in the face, but she left the
little child that she adored to be your comfort.
Mr. Mannering, you will come with me to that
poor woman's grave, and you will forgive her.
She gave you up what was most dear to her in
life."

He shook his head. " She had others that
were more dear to her."

" I could find it in my heart, if I were you, to
hope that it was so ; but I do not believe it.
How could she look you in the face again, having
sinned against you ?   But she left you what she
loved most. ' Dora, Dora,' was all her cry : but
she put Dora out of her arms for you.   Think
kindly of her, man !   A woman loves nothing on
this earth," cried Miss Bethune with passion,
" like the little child that has come from her, and

is of her, flesh of her flesh, bone of her bone : and she gave that over to you. She must have been a woman more just than most other women," Miss Bethune said.

Mr. Mannering made no reply. Perhaps he did not understand or believe in that definition of what a woman loves best ; but he thought of the passion of the other woman before him, and of the long hunger of her heart, with nothing to solace her, nothing to divert her thoughts from that hopeless loss and vacancy, nothing to compensate her for the ruin of her life. She had been a spirit in prison, shut up as in an iron cage, and she had borne it and not uttered even a cry. All three, or rather all four, of these lives, equally shipwrecked, came before him. His own stricken low in what would have been the triumph of another man ; his wife's, turned in a moment from such second possibilities of happiness as he could not yet bear to think of, and from the bliss of her child, into shame and guilt such as did not permit her to look her husband in the face, but drove her into exile and renunciation. And then this other pair. The woman with her secret romance, and long, long penitence and punishment. The man (whom she condemned yet more bitterly, perhaps with better cause than he had condemned his wife), a fugitive too, disappearing from country and home with the infant who died, or who did not die. What a round of dreadful mistake, mis-apprehension, rashness, failure! And who was he that he should count himself more badly treated than other men?

Miss Bethune thus gave him no *coup de grace.* She helped him after the prick of revival, to another more steadfast philosophy, in the com-parison of his fate with that of others. He saw with very clear eyes her delusion—that Harry Gordon was no son of hers, and that she would be compelled to acknowledge this and go back to the

dreariness and emptiness of her life, accepting the
dead baby as all that ever was hers : and he was
sorry for her to the bottom of his heart ; while she,
full of her illusions, went back to her own apartment full of pity for him, to whom Dora did not
make up for everything as Harry, she felt triumph-
antly, did to herself.

Dr. Roland watched them both, more concerned
for Mannering, who had been ill, than for Miss
Bethune, who had all that curious elasticity which
makes a woman generally so much more the
servant of her emotions than a man, often, in fact,
so much less affected by them. But there still
remained in the case of the patient another fiery
trial to go through, which still kept the doctor on
the alert and anxiously watching the course of
events. Mannering had said nothing of Dora's
fortune, of the money which he had refused
vehemently for her, but which he had no right to
refuse, and upon which, as Dr. Roland was aware,

she had already drawn.   One ordeal had passed, and had done no harm, but this other was still to come.

It came a day or two after, when Dr. Roland sat by Mannering's side after his return from the Museum, holding his pulse, and investigating in every way the effect upon him of the day's confinement.   It was evening, and the day had been hot and fatiguing.   Mr. Mannering was a little tired of this medical inspection, which occurred every evening.   He drew his wrist out of the doctor's hold, and turned the conversation abruptly to a new subject.

"There are a number of papers which I cannot find," he said, almost sharply, to Dora, with a meaning which immediately seemed to make the air tingle.   He had recovered his usual looks in a remarkable degree, and had even a little colour in his cheek.   His head was not drooping, nor his eye dim.   The stoop of a man occupied all day

among books seemed to have disappeared. He
leaned back in his chair a little, perhaps, but not
forward, as is the habit of weakness, and was not
afraid to look the doctor in the face. Dora stood
near him, alarmed, in the attitude of one about to
flee. She was eager to leave him with the doctor,
of whom he could ask no such difficult questions.

" Papers, father ? What papers ? " she said,
with an air of innocence which perhaps was a little
overdone.

" My business affairs are not so extensive," he
said, with a faint smile ; "and both you, doctor,
who really are the author of the extravagance,
and Dora, who is too young to meddle with such
matters, know all about them. My bills !—
Heaven knows they are enough to scare a poor
man : but they must be found. They were all
there a few days ago, now I can't find them.
Bring them, Dora. I must make a composition
with my creditors," he said, again, with that

forced and uncomfortable smile. Then he added, with some impatience : " My dear, do what I tell you, and do it at once ".

It was an emergency which Dora had been looking forward to, but that did not make it less terrible when it came. She stood very upright, holding by the table.

" The bills ? I don't know where to find them," she said, growing suddenly very red, and then very pale.

" Dora !" cried her father, in a warning tone. Then he added, with an attempt at banter : " Never mind the doctor. The doctor is in it ; he ought to pay half. We will take his advice. How small a dividend will content our creditors for the present ? Make haste, and do not lose any more time."

Dora stood her ground without wavering. " I cannot find them, father," she said.

" You cannot find them ? Nonsense ! This

is for my good, I suppose, lest I should not be able to bear it. My dear, your father declines to be managed for his good."

" I have not got them," said Dora firmly, but very pale. " I don't know where to find them; I don't want to find them, if I must say it, father, —not to manage you, but on my own account."

He raised himself upright too, and looked at her. Their eyes shone with the same glow; the two faces bore a strange resemblance,—his, the lines refined and softened by his illness; hers, every curve straightened and strengthened by force of passionate feeling.

" Father," said Dora almost fiercely, " I am not a child!"

" You are not a child?" A faint smile came over his face. " You are curiously like one," he said; " but what has that got to do with it?"

" Mannering, she is quite right. You ought to let her have her own way."

A cloud crossed Mr. Mannering's face. He was a mild man, but he did not easily brook interference. He made a slight gesture, as if throwing the intruder off.

"Father," said Dora again, "I have been the mistress of everything while you have been ill. You may say the doctor has done it, or Miss Bethune has done it,—they were very kind friends, and told me what to do,—but it was only your own child that had the right to do things for you, and the real person was me. I was a little girl when you began to be ill, but I am not so now. I've had to act for myself, father," the girl cried, the colour flaming back into her pale cheeks, "I've had to be responsible for a great many things; you can't take that from me, for it had to be. And you have not got a bill in the world."

He sat staring at her, half angry, half admiring, amazed by the change, the development; and yet to find her in her impulsive, childish vehemence exactly the same.

"They're all gone," cried Dora, with that dreadful womanish inclination to cry which spoils so many a fine climax. "I had a right to them— they were mine all through, and not yours. Father, even Fiddler! I've given you a present of that big book, which I almost broke my arm (if it had not been for Harry Gordon) carrying back. And now I know it's quarter day, and you're quite well off. Father, now I'm your little girl again, to do what you like and go where you like, and never, never hear a word of this more," cried Dora, flinging herself upon his shoulder, with her arms round his neck, in a paroxysm of tenderness and tears.

What was the man to do or say? He had uttered a cry of pain and shame, and something like fury; but with the girl clinging round his neck, sobbing, flung upon his mercy, he was helpless.

He looked over Dora's bright head at Dr. Roland with, notwithstanding his impatience of interference, a sort of appeal for help. However keen the pang was both to his heart and his pride, he could not throw off his only child from her shelter in his arms. After a moment his hand instinctively came upon her hair, smoothing it down, soothing her, though half against his will. The other arm, with which he had half put her away, stole round her with a softer pressure. His child, his only child, all of his, belonging to no one but him, and weeping her heart out upon his neck, altogether thrown upon him to be excused and pardoned for having given him all the tendance and care and help which it was in her to give. He looked at Roland with a half appeal, yet with that unconscious pride of superiority in the man who has, towards the man who has not.

"She has the right," said the doctor, himself

moved, but not perhaps with any sense of inferiority, for though he was nearly as old as Mr. Mannering, the beatitude of having a daughter had not yet become an ideal bliss to him—"she has the right; if anybody in the world has it, she has it, Mannering, and though she is a child, she has a heart and judgment as good as any of us. You'll have to let her do in certain matters what seemeth good in her own eyes."

Mr. Mannering shook his head, and then bent it in reluctant acquiescence with a sigh.

CHAPTER XXV.

THE house in Bloomsbury became vacant and silent.

The people who had given it interest and importance were dispersed and gone. Dr. Roland only remained, solitary and discontented, feeling himself cast adrift in the world, angry at the stillness overhead, where the solid foot of Gilchrist no longer made the floor creak, or the lighter step of her mistress sent a thrill of energy and life through it; but still more angry when new lodgers came, and new steps sounded over the carpet, which, deprived of all Miss Bethune's rugs, was thin and poor. The doctor thought of changing his lodging himself, in the depression of that change; but it is a serious matter for a doctor to change his abode, and Janie's anæmia was becoming a serious case, and wanted more looking after than ever would be given to it were he out of the way. So he consented to the inevitable, and remained. Mrs. Simcox had to refurnish the second floor, when all Mr. Mannering's pretty furniture and his books were taken away, and did it very badly, as was natural, and got "a couple" for her lodgers, who were quite satisfied with second-hand mahogany and hair-cloth. Dr. Roland looked at the new lodgers when he met them with eyes blank, and a total absence of interest: but beginning soon to see that the stock market was telling upon the first floor, and that the lady on the second had a cough, he began to allow himself a little to be shaken out of his indifference. They might, however, be objects of professional interest, but no more. The Mannerings were abroad. After that great flash in the pan of a return to the Museum, Nature had reclaimed her rights, and

Mr. Mannering had been obliged to apply for a prolonged leave, which by degrees led to retirement and a pension.   Miss Bethune had returned to her native country, and to the old house near the Highland line which belonged to her.   Vague rumours that she was not Miss Bethune at all, but a married lady all the time, had reached Bloomsbury; but nobody knew, as Mrs. Simcox said, what were the rights of the case.

In a genial autumn, some years after the above events, Dr. Roland, who had never ceased to keep a hold upon his former neighbours, whose departure had so much saddened his life, arrived on a visit at that Highland home.   It was a rambling house, consisting of many additions and enlargements built on to the original fabric of a small, strait, and high semi-fortified dwelling-place, breathing that air of austere and watchful defence which lingers about some old houses, though the parlours of the eighteenth century,

not to say the drawing-rooms of the nineteenth,
with their broad open windows, accessible from
the ground, were strangely unlike the pointed
tall gable with its crow steps, and the high post
of watchfulness up among the roofs, the little
balcony or terrace which swept the horizon on
every side. There Miss Bethune, still Miss
Bethune, abode in the fulness of a life which
sought no further expansion, among her own
people. She had called to her a few of the most
ancient and trusted friends of the family on her
first arrival there, and had disclosed to them her
secret story, and asked their advice. She had
never borne her husband's name. There had
been no break, so far as any living person except
Gilchrist was aware, in the continuity of her life.
The old servants were dead, and the old minister,
who had been coaxed and frightened into per-
forming a furtive ceremony. No one except
Gilchrist was aware of any of those strange events

which had gone on in the maze of little rooms and crooked passages. Miss Bethune was strong in the idea of disclosing everything when she returned home. She meant to publish her strange and painful story among her friends and to the world at large, and to acknowledge and put in his right place, as she said, her son. A small knot of grave county gentlemen sat upon the matter, and had all the evidence placed before them in order to decide this question.

Harry Gordon himself was the first to let them know that his claims were more than doubtful— that they were, in fact, contradicted by his own recollections and everything he really knew about himself; and Mr. Templar brought his report, which made it altogether impossible to believe in the relationship. But Miss Bethune's neighbours soon came to perceive that these were nothing to her own fervid conviction, which they only made stronger the oftener the objections were repeated.

She would not believe that part of Mr. Templar's story which concerned the child ; there was no documentary proof. The husband's death could be proved, but it was not even known where that of the unfortunate baby had taken place, and nothing could be ascertained about it. She took no notice of the fact that her husband and Harry Gordon's father had neither died at the same place nor at the same time. As it actually happened, there was sufficient analogy between time and place to make it possible to imagine, had there been no definite information, that they were the same person. And this was more than enough for Miss Bethune. She was persuaded at last, however, by the unanimous judgment of the friends she trusted, to depart from her first intention, to make no scandal in the countryside by changing her name, and to leave her property to Harry, describing him as a relation by the mother's side. "It came to you by will, not in direct inheritance," the chief of these gentlemen of the county said. " Let it go to him in the same way. We all respect the voice of nature, and you are not a silly woman, my dear Janet, to believe a thing that is not : but the evidence would not bear investigation in a court of law. He is a fine young fellow, and has spoken out like a gentleman."

"As he has a good right—the last of the Bethunes, as well as a Gordon of no mean name !"

" Just so," said the convener of the county ; "there is nobody here that will not give him his hand. But you have kept the secret so long, it is my opinion you should keep it still. We all know—all that are worth considering—and what is the use of making a scandal and an outcry among all the silly auld wives of the countryside ? And leave him your land by will, as the nearest relation you care to acknowledge on his mother's side."

This was the decision that was finally come to ; and Miss Bethune was not less a happy mother, nor Harry Gordon the less a good son, that the relationship between them was quite beyond the reach of proof, and existed really in the settled conviction of one brain alone. The delusion made her happy, and it gave him a generous reason for acquiescing in the change so much to his advantage which took place in his life.

The Mannerings arrived at Beaton Castle shortly after the doctor, on their return from the Continent. Dora was now completely woman-grown, and had gradually and tacitly taken the command of her father and all his ways. He had been happy in the certainty that when he left off work and consented to take that long rest, it was his own income upon which they set out—an income no longer encumbered with any debts to pay, even for old books. He had gone on happily

upon that conviction ever since; they had tra-
velled a great deal together, and he had com
pletely recovered his health, and in a great degree
his interest, both in science and life. He had
even taken up those studies which had been interrupted by the shipwreck of his happiness, and
the breaking up of his existence, and had recently
published some of the results of them, with a
sudden lighting up once again of the fame of the
more youthful Mannering, from whom such great
things had been expected. The more he had
become interested in work and the pursuits of
knowledge, the less he had known or thought of
external affairs ; and for a long time Dora had
acted very much as she pleased, increasing such
luxuries as he liked, and encouraging every one
of the extravagances into which, when left to
himself, he naturally fell. Sometimes still he
would pause over an expensive book, with a half
hesitation, half apology.

"But perhaps we cannot afford it. I ought not to give myself so many indulgences, Dora."

"You know how little we spend, father," Dora would say,—"no house going on at home to swallow up the money. We live for next to nothing here." And he received her statement with implicit faith.

Thus both the elder personages of this history were deceived, and found a great part of their happiness in it. Was it a false foundation of happiness, and wrong in every way, as Dr. Roland maintained? He took these two young people into the woods, and read them the severest of lessons.

"You are two lies," he said; "you are deceiving two people who are of more moral worth than either of you. It is probably not your fault, but that of some wicked grandmother; but you ought to be told it, all the same. And I don't say that I blame you. I daresay I should do it also in your case. But it's a shame, all the same."

" In the case of my—mistress, my friend, my all but mother," said young Gordon, with some emotion, "the deceit is all her own. I have said all I could say, and so have her friends. We have proved to her that it could not be I, everything has been put before her; and if she determines, after all that, that I am the man, what can I do? I return her affection for affection cordially, for who was ever so good to any one as she is to me? And I serve her as her son might do. I am of use to her actually, though you may not think it. And why should I try to wound her heart, by reasserting that I am not what she thinks, and that she is deceived? I do my best to satisfy, not to deceive her. Therefore, do not say it; I am no lie."

" All very well and very plausible," said the doctor, "but in no wise altering my opinion.

And, Miss Dora, what have you got to say?"

"I say nothing," said Dora; "there is no deceit at all. If you only knew how particular I am! Father's income suffices for himself; he is not in debt to any one. He has a good income —a very good income—four hundred a year, enough for any single man. Don't you think so? I have gone over it a great many times, and I am sure he does not spend more than that—not so much; the calculation is all on paper. Do you remember teaching me to do accounts long ago? I am very good at it now. Father is not bound to keep me, when there are other people who will keep on sending me money: and he has quite enough—too much for himself; then where is the deceit, or shame either? My conscience is quite clear."

"You are two special pleaders," the doctor said; "you are too many for me when you are together. I'll get you apart, and convince you of your sin. And what," he cried suddenly, taking them by surprise, " my fine young sir and madam, would happen if either one or other of you took it into your heads to marry ? That is what I should like to know."

They looked at each other for a moment as it were in a flash of crimson light, which seemed to fly instantaneously from one to another. They looked first at him, and then exchanged one lightning glance, and then each turned a little aside on either side of the doctor. Was it to hide that something which was nothing, that spontaneous, involuntary momentary interchange of looks, from his curious eyes ? Dr. Roland was struck as by that harmless lightning. He, the expert, had forgotten what contagion there might be in the air. They were both tall, both fair, two slim figures in their youthful grace, embodiments of all that was hopeful, strong, and lifelike. The doctor had not taken into consideration certain effects known to all men which are not in the books. "Whew-ew!" he breathed in a long whistle of astonishment, and said no more.

9

THE END.

www.ingramcontent.com/pod-product-compliance
Lightning Source LLC
Chambersburg PA
CBHW031426020726
47499CB00005B/1620